WITHDRAWN

STACKS

3-22

Out There

WITHDRAWN

Out There

STORIES

Kate Folk

RANDOM HOUSE

New York

Out There is a work of fiction. Names, characters, places, and incidents are the products of the author's imagination or are used fictitiously. Any resemblance to actual events, locales, or persons, living or dead, is entirely coincidental.

Copyright © 2022 by Kate Folk

All rights reserved.

Published in the United States by Random House, an imprint and division of Penguin Random House LLC, New York.

RANDOM HOUSE and the HOUSE colophon are registered trademarks of Penguin Random House LLC.

The following stories were previously published in different form: "Out There" in *The New Yorker;* "The Last Woman on Earth" in *Prairie Schooner;* "Heart Seeks Brain" in *Conjunctions;* "The Void Wife" in *Gulf Coast;* "Shelter" in *Zyzzyva;* "The Head in the Floor" in *Tupelo Quarterly;* "Tahoe" in *Joyland;* "The Bone Ward" in *McSweeney's Quarterly Concern;* "Doe Eyes" in *Hayden's Ferry Review;* "The House's Beating Heart" in *Tin House Flash Fridays;* "A Scale Model of Gull Point" in *Granta;* "Dating a Somnambulist" in *Hobart;* and "The Turkey Rumble" in *Word Riot.*

LIBRARY OF CONGRESS CATALOGING-IN-PUBLICATION DATA
Names: Folk, Kate, author.
Title: Out there : stories / Kate Folk.
Description: New York : Random House, [2022]
Identifiers: LCCN 2021020521 (print) | LCCN 2021020522 (ebook) |
ISBN 9780593231463 (hardcover ; acid-free paper) | ISBN 9780593231470 (ebook)
Subjects: LCGFT: Short stories.
Classification: LCC PS3606.O446 O88 2022 (print) | LCC PS3606.O446 (ebook) |
DDC 813/.6—dc23
LC record available at https://lccn.loc.gov/2021020521
LC ebook record available at https://lccn.loc.gov/2021020522

Printed in Canada on acid-free paper

randomhousebooks.com

9 8 7 6 5 4 3 2 1

First Edition

Designed by Debbie Glasserman

For my parents

Contents

Out There 3

The Last Woman on Earth 34

Heart Seeks Brain 39

The Void Wife 45

Shelter 53

The Head in the Floor 80

Tahoe 85

The Bone Ward 89

Doe Eyes 125

The House's Beating Heart 137

A Scale Model of Gull Point 141

Dating a Somnambulist 158

Moist House 162

The Turkey Rumble 188

Big Sur 195

Acknowledgments 243

Out There

Out There

was putting myself out there. On my return to San Francisco from a gloomy Thanksgiving with my mother in Illinois, I downloaded Tinder, Bumble, and a few other dating apps I'd seen Instagram ads for. I was thirty, too young to accept a life void of excitement, romance, and perhaps, eventually, the lively antics of a child. I resolved to pass judgment on several hundred men per day, and to make an effort to message the few I matched with. I was picky enough that this seemed not wholly absurd. It would be like a new workout routine, a daily regimen to forestall a future of more permanent aloneness, and enjoy my relative youth in the meantime.

I'd never liked the idea of finding a romantic partner on

an app, the same way you'd order pizza or an Uber. Such a method seemed to reduce love to another transaction. I had always felt it catered to lazy, unimaginative people. A worthy man would be out in the world doing things, not swiping on women's pictures in his dim apartment, like a coward. To further complicate matters, it was estimated that men on dating apps in the city were now 50 percent blots. But what choice did I have? Apps seemed to be the way everyone found each other these days. After my last breakup, I spent a while "letting something happen," which meant doing nothing. Years passed and nothing did happen, and I realized that without my intervention, my hand pushing against the warm back of fate, it was possible nothing ever would. In the end, it seemed to come down to never dating again, or taking the chance of being blotted. Though I supposed there had always been risks.

The early blots had been easy to identify. They were too handsome, for one thing. Their skin was smooth and glowing, and they were uniformly tall and lean. Jawlines you could cut bread with. They were the best-looking men in any room, and had no sense of humor.

I met one of these early blots several years ago. My friend Peter had invited me to a dinner party hosted by a tech founder he'd grown up with in the Sunset District, and with whom he'd once followed the band Phish around the country, selling nitrous and poppers to concertgoers. Peter and I didn't really hang out, beyond the meetings we attended in church basements for people who no longer drank. But I was bored, and it was a free dinner, and Peter made it sound like he'd already asked a bunch of other people who'd said no, which took some of the pressure off.

At dinner, I sat next to a guy named Roger. He had the telltale blot look—high forehead, lush hair, shapely eyebrows—but I didn't recognize him for what he was, because the blot phenomenon hadn't yet been exposed. Roger was solicitous, asking about my family, my work as a teacher, and my resentment toward the tech industry. When I declined the server's offer of wine, Roger's golden eyes flared with recognition, and he asked if I was in recovery. I said yes, for five years at that point, and he nodded gravely, saying he admired my commitment to this lifestyle; his dear aunt was also sober.

Roger seemed eager to charm, but I was not charmed. I felt spotlighted by his attentiveness, his anticipation of what I might want—another helping of fava bean salad, more water, an extra napkin when I dropped a chunk of braised pork on my skirt. I would say something self-deprecating, and he'd regard me steadily and assure me that I was a wonderful person, deserving of all I wanted from life, which wasn't what I'd been asking for. Roger didn't know me and wasn't a credible judge of my worth—unless his position was that all people had worth, which made him no judge at all. When I shifted the subject to him, he supplied a backstory that seemed pre-written.

"I came from ranchland in the northern United States," he told me. "My father was stern but loving, in his way. My mother is a wonderful woman who raised the four of us into strong, capable adults. My childhood was not without hardship, but these adversities shaped me into the person I am today. Now I live in the San Francisco Bay Area, land of innovation and possibility. I am grateful for the life I've been given, and I know it is thanks to the people who have loved and supported me on the journey."

I forced a chuckle of acknowledgment. "Wow," I said. "That's great."

As I drove Peter back to the Richmond District in my decrepit Corolla, he revealed that his friend, the event's host, had sprinkled the dinner party with blots.

"Blots?"

"It's an acronym for something," Peter said. "They're biomorphic humanoids. The latest advancement in the field of tactile illusion." He paused. "Fake people," he added.

I concealed my shock, not wanting to give Peter the satisfaction. "So you invited me to be the subject of a Turing test for some company's new product, without compensation," I said.

"You got a free dinner, didn't you?"

"Well, he was boring," I said. "And too handsome. I hate guys like that."

"Handsome guys?"

"Yeah. I'm not attracted to them."

Peter said he hoped I'd written all this on the comment card that had been distributed with the gelato, which asked me to rate my dinner companions' various attributes. I'd given Roger all fives, out of habit, and in retrospect I was glad not to have aided the blot revolution with my honest feedback.

The blots were originally designed to perform caretaking jobs that necessitated a high level of empathy. They were meant to work in hospices and elder-care centers, tending to people who were suffering and who would soon die. Such jobs were typically low-paying, and it would be better, more ethical, so the thinking went, to place blots in those roles. They would do a fine job, and then after a few months they'd dematerialize, their corporeal presence dissipating into a cloud of vapor.

But aside from a few elite facilities, hospitals weren't able to invest in the blot program, which was prohibitively expensive and unpopular among donors. The families who could afford top-flight medical care didn't like the idea of their loved ones being cared for by blots, even when it was shown that blots performed these tasks more effectively than humans. Soon blot technology was appropriated by a Russian company, and blots were employed in illegal activities—most commonly, identity fraud. Blots began using dating apps to target vulnerable women. It happened to my friend Alicia, last summer.

"Friend" is a term I use loosely. Alicia was someone I knew from the recovery community. We sometimes went out for food after a meeting, and it was on such an occasion, six months ago, that Alicia told us about her experience with a blot named Steve. I already suspected Alicia had been blotted, because her Facebook profile had engaged me in eerie conversation a few weeks earlier. *I have always admired your shoes,* she messaged me, late one night, and I thought at first that she'd relapsed and was taking the opportunity to insult me.

Five of us were out at a diner on Geary, a place we liked even though the food was overpriced and bad. Alicia ordered a chocolate milkshake—like a child, I thought—and recounted the ordeal. Steve had proposed they go on a weekend trip to Big Sur, after just a few weeks of dating. This was textbook blot, a red flag Alicia should have recognized. Blots always wanted to go to Big Sur, where cell service was spotty, to give themselves some lead time with the victim's data. They'd lavish a woman with praise, rich food, and vigorous sex, and then in the middle of the night they'd steal the data stored in her phone, copy her credit card info, and disappear with a voluptuous "bloop" sound, like a raindrop hitting the floor of a metal bucket, a cloud of lavender-scented vapor all that remained.

"I woke up and he was gone," Alicia said. "The room smelled great, though."

Alicia canceled her credit cards immediately, but the blot had hacked her laptop and changed all her passwords. It took months to untangle Steve's work. His tactics were vindictive, and strangely intimate. He'd sent personalized emails to everyone in her contact lists, exploiting every scrap of personal information Alicia had divulged over the weeks they'd dated. On her Facebook page, he posted provocative selfies she'd sent to him or kept on her phone. We had all seen these photos—Alicia, in a lace bralette and thong, posing in a full-length mirror in the dingy shared bathroom of her apartment, her back arched at what looked like a painful angle to showcase her ass.

At the diner, Alicia framed herself as a woman with a hard-won ounce of wisdom. "If it seems too good to be true, it probably is," she said, then kept sucking air through her milkshake straw. I nodded along with the others, thinking that Alicia was an idiot. Steve had not even done a good job of concealing his blot identity, and she'd fallen for it anyway, clinging to the hope that her time had finally come.

Blot technology continued to advance. They were now said to be programmed with more complex psychological profiles, overt flaws, and varied physical characteristics, which made detection increasingly difficult. Blots were always male, because their original creators believed that male blots would more easily convey authority, minimizing the risk of sexual exploitation by unscrupulous hospital employees. I didn't want to join Alicia among the ranks of the blotted, so I was vigilant as I chatted with men on the apps.

A few weeks into my new routine, I matched with Sam. His profile was brief and inoffensive, referencing his love of yoga, backpacking, and seeing live music. He worked for a tech company, something about firewalls. I wasn't sure what those were, and he didn't care to explain. *It's just a job*, he wrote, then changed the subject to bands he wanted to see.

On our first date, we went to a Thai restaurant near my house. Sam was tall and reasonably attractive, but not in the polished, male-model blot way. His body was thick, shoulders broad beneath his black denim jacket. His brown hair reached his shoulders, and his face was covered in a patchy beard that seemed incidental, as if he'd simply run out of razors one day and been too lazy to buy more.

Sam brooded over the menu. I proposed that we split curry and noodles, and he agreed, seeming relieved to have the burden of deciding removed. After we ordered, he provided a cursory sketch of his childhood in Wisconsin, at my prompting. His account was less eloquent than Roger's had been, and this helped assure me of its authenticity. He lingered over his brother, who had quit law school and now worked as a salmon fisherman in Alaska. "He always went his own way," Sam said, with admiration and perhaps a touch of resentment. Sam had remained in Wisconsin, near their family. He'd finished a master's degree in computer science at UW–Madison, then broken off an engagement to his long-time girlfriend; when I asked why they'd split, he said only that they'd begun dating too young and had grown apart over the years. He'd moved to San Francisco eight months ago, seeking a new start.

I told Sam that I'd lived in the city for ten years, and waited for him to ask why I'd moved here. But then our food came, and the thread was lost. This had happened several times while we were messaging on the app—I would drop some reference to my life, and Sam would fail to ask a logical follow-up question. I savored these instances of human selfishness. Even if the new generation of blots had more flaws than the old ones, I figured they'd still be primed to retrieve any breadcrumb of a woman's past that might help them more thoroughly fuck her over when the time came. Sam's inattention was a kind of freedom. I could say anything, and he'd simply nod, and a moment later begin talking about something else.

In the past I had approached dating with the typical fervor of an addict. I'd worked independently to construct the scaffolding of a relationship, then waited for the man I was seeing to step into the blank space I'd retained in his form. Inevitably, he would either balk at the role I'd assigned him, or accede to my formidable will, at which point I'd realize I didn't really want him as my boyfriend anyway. With Sam, I resolved to do nothing. I would root myself in the present moment, accepting the man before me without judgment. I allowed Sam to set the pace of our dating, waiting for him to initiate contact and propose when we should hang out next.

On our third date, I invited him back to my apartment after dinner, and we had sex. Sam handled my body thoughtfully, like a new pair of shoes he would break in and wear often. It was not mind-blowing, but early sex rarely was. It wasn't horrifyingly bad, and in this I glimpsed limitless potential. He was careful with his weight and with where he placed his knees. I liked how, as he hovered his body above mine, he cupped the side of my face in his hand.

That first night, as I lay in the dark with my arm slung across Sam's chest, I waited for the old void-opening feeling to take me, the particular loneliness of lying next to another person. But for once, this sadness didn't arrive. It felt good having Sam there, as if the last puzzle piece had been set into place. For the first time in years, my apartment was full. The cats, who usually slept on the bed with me, had been displaced to alternate positions in the apartment. I sensed their presence out in the dark, on the chair or the couch or in the closet. Sam had petted them for a while when he arrived. He'd allowed one cat to bite his hand gently, the other to drool on the thigh of his jeans. It was nice to have four mammals under one roof, each of us trusting the others not to kill us while we slept. This was the appeal, I thought, of a family. This was what everyone had been going on about all these years.

———

On Monday, I went to work as usual, though the plates of my life had shifted. I was dating someone now. My senses felt heightened as I biked down Market Street in the morning. I saw the world through the eyes of a recently fucked woman.

I was a teacher, of sorts. I'd had the same two part-time jobs for years, for a private ESL school and a for-profit art university that did heavy recruiting in China. In the mornings, I taught Upper-Intermediate English to a class of fourteen students in a narrow, orange-walled room, located on the fifteenth floor of a glass skyscraper on Montgomery Street. The students were in their late teens and early twenties, mostly from Switzerland, South Korea, and Saudi Arabia. The roster changed from week to week. There was no sense of continuity or progression toward an end point. We worked through the proprietary textbook, then started again at the beginning.

In the afternoon, I'd head south of Market to one of the art classes for which I was providing what the college termed "language support." I took notes while the instructor lectured on fashion design or computer animation or art history. After the lecture, I would wait for the international students to ask for my help—to explain difficult vocabulary and American colloquialisms, providing a verbal Cliffs Notes of what we'd just heard—but they rarely did.

I moved through that Monday in a neurochemical fog. I'd been single long enough that my tendrils of attachment had dried up and ceased issuing their commands. Now they'd been activated again, and I wondered how I had ever cared

about anything other than sex. The students no longer annoyed me; they now seemed righteous, bristling with youthful energy. They, too, were probably horny, and resentful at
having to sit through class when they could be fucking and
exploring the city. I resisted the urge to text Sam. My single
years had made me strong, and I was determined not to sabo-
tage this new relationship with my insecurity. I would wait
for Sam to make contact, even if it took several days. I accepted the possibility that he'd never contact me again. Perhaps he would turn out to be a blot, or simply a man who
didn't want a relationship. Such uncertainty was the nature
of existence. We brought things into our lives, and time
passed. Things exited our lives. That was about all that ever
happened.

I didn't tell my friends about Sam right away. It was going
well, which I knew they would take as an ominous sign. I had
opened myself to the possibility of being blotted, and I didn't
want to hear my misgivings echoed by others.

When Sam and I had been dating a month, I was out at
the diner after our Tuesday meeting with Peter, Kevin, and
Dan. All three men were in their forties, and single. Dan told
us about a neighbor he'd been sleeping with; she now expected to come over every night to watch TV, while Dan preferred to watch TV alone. Kevin asked if I'd been seeing
anyone, and I mentioned Sam, careful to downplay how invested I'd already become.

"You met him on Tinder?" Kevin said, skeptically.

"Yeah, but he's not a blot," I said. "He's very casual about
the whole thing."

"What does he look like?" Peter asked.

"I think he's attractive," I admitted. "But he's also kind of ugly. Not like a blot."

The men exchanged meaningful looks. It felt rude to talk about Sam's appearance, which implied I had also made aesthetic judgments about each of them at some point. There had been a moment, years ago, when I might have dated one of these guys. But then I got to know them, and it became impossible. You have to make your mistakes with people early on, when you first meet them, or the door slams shut. You forget there was ever a door to begin with.

"Does he have a car?" Peter said. Blots couldn't get driver's licenses; it was a sign all the articles mentioned.

"Well, no," I said. "But he doesn't need one. He takes BART."

"Have you seen his place?" Dan asked.

Sam lived in the Oakland Hills. I'd slept at his apartment once, on my insistence. He warned me to be silent as we descended the carpeted stairs to his room. He'd lived there only a month, and wasn't sure if having overnight guests was cool with his roommates. So I was asked to pretend I didn't exist, something I had plenty of practice with. It was a little degrading, which I took as another promising sign.

Sam slept in a sleeping bag wadded at the center of a king-sized bed. There was a closet in the hallway where he kept his camping gear, and from which he retrieved a spare pillow for me to sleep on, still in its wrapping, as if he'd bought it for this purpose. At the foot of the bed was a Rubbermaid container full of folded T-shirts and socks. On its lid sat an electric kettle he used to boil water for coffee, so he wouldn't have to go upstairs. He had done this the morning I woke up there.

We passed a single mug back and forth. I asked if he had any milk.

"I think there's some in the kitchen," he said. I waited for him to get the milk, but he continued sitting on the edge of his bed, drinking the coffee. I would have gotten it myself, but I was not supposed to betray my presence to his roommates.

In the diner, I highlighted this detail as evidence of Sam's humanity. "If he were a blot, he wouldn't act that way," I said. "He would jump at the opportunity to get milk for my coffee. They wouldn't program them to be completely selfish." I paused. "Would they?"

Kevin shook his head doubtfully. "I don't know, man," he said. "The technology keeps getting more advanced. You need to be careful."

"Maybe he isn't a blot," Dan said, standing and tossing a twenty onto the plastic tray that held our check. "He might just be kind of a dick."

The early blots didn't live anywhere. They stalked the streets and the park all night, waiting for their next date. There were still some of them out there, blots who'd never managed to attach to a host. The company that unleashed them had apparently forgotten, or didn't care, leaving them to wander eternally, like those electric scooters you'd see abandoned on sidewalks. Sometimes I would pass one on the street, his eyes wild and blank, his clothes rumpled, his skin and hair still perfect. I felt a little sorry for these lost blots. It must have been painful to be designed for one purpose, and to find yourself unable to complete it.

Once I'd seen Sam's place, I was satisfied. We never stayed there again, as my apartment was objectively better. I would clean the day he was coming over, and always made sure I had eggs and coffee for the morning. Before we went to bed, Sam would place his selvedge jeans and horsehide boots on a high shelf in my closet behind the mirrored door, so the cats wouldn't scratch them. I had never known my cats to scratch shoes or clothes, but I didn't want to insist on their harmlessness, in case I was wrong about them.

I allowed Sam to take his protective measures, and in turn, I took mine. I slept with my laptop placed on the shelf built into the wall on my side of the bed, my phone tucked under my pillow. I locked my devices with passcodes, though it was documented that blots were able to hack these codes anyway. If Sam tried to reach over me for my laptop, I was sure to wake up. I was a light sleeper, naturally anxious, especially with a new man sleeping next to me. Not that we slept much when Sam stayed over. We usually had sex two or three times, then again in the morning. Each round yielded diminishing returns. Sometimes, toward the end, Sam couldn't come at all, and I would feel satisfied, like I'd drained a reservoir. I imagined emptying Sam so that I could fill him up again with something else.

Weeks passed, and Sam and I fell into a routine approximating a relationship. I continued letting him take the lead. I lived for the one weekend night we'd go out for dinner, then head back to my apartment and have sex. One Sunday morning, when Sam was on his way out my door, I proposed we get dinner on a weeknight. He kissed my cheek and told me he'd check his schedule, but the week progressed without him mentioning it, and it seemed too pushy for me to ask again. I reminded myself that anything I held too tightly would slip from my grasp like sand.

On Monday I'd return to work, desolate in the knowledge that it would be a full week before I saw Sam again. In the mornings I guided students through pointless games they hated, then went over the answers to homework they hadn't done. In the afternoons I lurked in the back of various class-rooms, grinning at students when they returned from the restroom. They would smile uncomfortably and look away, as if I were an embarrassing relative.

On a Wednesday, I was bored enough during a three-hour fashion-design class that I dared to text Sam first. I was re-lieved he hadn't proposed a trip to Big Sur, but I'd been think-ing it might be nice to go somewhere else. There was a long weekend coming up in a few weeks.

I sent the text—*Prez Day soon! Any interest in a weekend getaway?*—and returned to my notebook. I always took me-ticulous notes during the instructor's lecture, but everything after that, while the students worked individually on their design projects, was gibberish I'd written in an attempt to look occupied. Each day's notes slid precipitously from coher-ence to nonsense, as though I were suffering from a mood disorder.

Sounds good, Sam had texted, when I next checked my phone.

Great! I replied. *Where should we go?*

I regretted this text immediately. Sam might feel pressured by my eagerness and withdraw. Sure enough, he didn't write back for three hours. *Let's play it by ear,* he finally replied. *Still plenty of time.*

My friends agreed this was a good sign. "If he was a blot, he'd be wanting to lock it down," Peter said through a cloud of nicotine vapor, as we stood on the sidewalk after a meeting. I was reassured by Peter's confidence, though I no longer really feared that Sam was a blot. We'd been dating two months now. Blots were known to achieve their aim within the first month of dating. Anything longer simply wasn't cost-effective.

I knew that Peter, along with everyone else, was surprised by this turn I had taken. I'd gained appeal in their view, succeeding where they had failed. I was approaching the relationship realistically. I was not using Sam as human fodder to stuff into the emptiness my addiction once filled. Friends began asking me for advice on their own dating lives. Remain in the present, I counseled. Don't be attached to outcomes. Accept people exactly as they are, in this moment.

On the Sunday before Presidents' Day weekend, Sam sat on my loveseat, eating the eggs I had made, while I sat at my desk by the window with my own plate. He'd retrieved his clothes from my closet and put them back on, a black T-shirt with a shallow V-neck and his Japanese selvedge jeans. I knew that in another twenty minutes, he'd be gone. I didn't see how we could delay making a plan for the trip any longer.

"So," I said carefully. "Where should we go next weekend?"

"Oh, right," Sam said, as if he hadn't been thinking about it at all. "Let's check the weather."

I got out my laptop and joined him on the loveseat. A weather site projected a solid wall of rain for the entire coastal region, starting on Tuesday and continuing through the following week. This would make camping difficult, unless we drove to the desert, which I doubted the Corolla would be up for. It was the first time I had opened my laptop in Sam's presence. I kept waiting for him to grab it, but he maintained a respectful distance, suggesting terms I might search for.

We considered alternatives to camping, and landed on some hot springs up north. I'd heard about this no-frills resort from friends, a place where swimsuits were optional and guests cooked their meals in a communal kitchen. Sam made the call, using his credit card for the three-night reservation, with the expectation that I would Venmo him my half. I listened as he slowly repeated his name to the person on the other end of the line. It was the first time I'd heard him speak his own last name aloud, and I was surprised by the way he pronounced it, the hard "a" that I'd assumed was soft.

After he hung up, Sam slung his arm around my shoulders and asked what my plans were for the day. Normally, he left right after eating the eggs I had made. I felt a clawing need to make him stay longer. "We could make juice," I proposed.

My juicer was heavy, made of mirrored steel with a rounded back. Over the years, it had accrued layers of romantic significance—first, the long-distance boyfriend who'd bought it for me, an older guy in Los Angeles who liked to send me presents, perhaps as a bulwark against my obvious ambivalence regarding our relationship. The juicer was an expensive model. Fruits, vegetables, herbs, whatever, went into a narrow spout at the top, to be mashed into a spinning cone using a beige stick. The juice came out the end, and the fibrous remnants fell out through the bottom.

When my LA boyfriend was in town, we made juice together. Then after we broke up, I used the juicer with subsequent partners. It made me a little sad, thinking of the different men I had juiced with, who had since exited the stage of my life. But now Sam and I were planning a trip together, a milestone that called for celebration.

There was a farmers' market a few blocks away, on Clement Street. The morning fog had burned off, and we walked to the market beneath a cold blue sky. We bought kale, green apples, celery, beets, and ginger, splitting the cost evenly. I watched Sam make small talk with the vendors. He spent several minutes asking a teenage boy about the different types of apple his family's orchard cultivated, and I felt proud, imagining the boy was impressed by Sam's masculine competence. Back in my kitchen, we washed the produce, cut it into pieces, and took turns feeding the pieces into the juicer and plunging down with the special stick.

We moved back into the main room with our glasses of tart, grainy juice. I felt a new ease unfurling between us, as if making juice had sealed us within a bubble of domesticity. I asked Sam to teach me how to pitch an imaginary baseball, knowing this request would gratify him. He often referenced his years as a left-handed pitcher in high school. He'd almost been recruited to a Division I school, whatever that meant, but was thwarted by a vindictive coach who refused to let him play the day the recruiters visited, for reasons I didn't quite understand.

We stood in the middle of my apartment, and Sam showed me how to turn my upper body, channeling my full energy into my pitching arm. I watched us in the mirrored wall that slid to expose my closet. As I drew my arm back for another fake pitch, I remembered my dad teaching me how to throw a ball, in our small backyard in the suburbs of Chicago; he'd taken pride in my not throwing "like a girl," though that was all I was.

I mentioned this to Sam, and before I could stop myself, I'd begun talking about my dad's descent into drug addiction, well under way the day he taught me to throw. We settled into the loveseat and I recounted the full story of my dad's diminishment. He'd disappear for weeks, then return in worse shape than before. He went to rehab at one point, and when he came back he'd grown a beard. I told Sam about the uncanny feeling of seeing my dad with a beard, as if he had been replaced by a similar man, the details slightly off, like when a TV show switches actors between seasons. I was fourteen then; it was the last time I saw him. For five years afterward, he sent me and my mom the occasional letter, full of apologies, along with promises that he was cleaning up his act and would be back with us soon. Eventually, the letters stopped coming, and my mom thought it was best we move on.

There was little emotion in my retelling; I'd told the story in therapy, and in meetings, and in the early stages of past relationships, at the juncture where I hoped they might become more serious. The feeling was sucked out, the bare facts remaining, like the fiber expelled by the juicer.

Sam listened attentively. When I finished, he placed his empty juice glass on the coffee table, cupped my face in his broad hand, and kissed me. It was a nice gesture, but it felt a bit affected, as if it had been lifted from a movie—some scene where a character reveals scars on her body, and the man gravely kisses each of them, confirming that he still accepts and desires her. I would have preferred for him to respond with a story of his own, to say anything, really. Still, I sensed I'd laid the groundwork for further revelation. I was used to getting to know people by learning about the painful experiences that had shaped them. I figured Sam simply needed more time.

For once, when Sam left my apartment, I didn't feel desolate in his absence. I felt we had forged a new intimacy, like a hot stone tucked at the base of my throat, keeping me warm.

The night before our trip, Sam slept over, and in the morning we drove north. It was raining as we crossed the Golden Gate Bridge, the view obscured by thick fog, as if the landscape resisted collaboration in the romantic narrative I'd spun around the trip. We stopped at a Trader Joe's in San Rafael, and ticked through items on the list we had made. As we waited in line with our cart, I imagined doing this with Sam, year after year. We would buy a house in some region where buying a house was possible. We would work in separate rooms, and bring each other juice. I would have what other people had after all, in a surprising twist of fate.

The resort was located east of Mendocino, accessed via narrow roads carved through dense forest. Sam had offered to drive on this last leg, and I sat tensely in the passenger seat, my old car feeling like a plastic toy that might crack apart.

We checked in at the lodge and located our guest room, one of the tiny freestanding cottages lining the gravel path to the pools. The door didn't lock. We were advised not to keep anything of value in our room, and I was happy to leave my phone in the trunk of my car. I'd planned to wear my swimsuit, but it was clear when we entered the locker room that a swimsuit would make a person stand out, in a bad way. Everyone used the pools naked. We saw them through the locker-room window, mostly couples and a few solo middle-aged men, strolling across the wet concrete. Judgment glimmered through me, a disdain for hippies, people who moved through the world with unwarranted confidence—a prejudice I hadn't known I harbored. I felt shy as I removed my clothes and stacked them in a locker; being naked with Sam in this context felt different from being naked with him in my apartment.

"Does this seem weird?" I whispered, on our way out of the locker room.

"Why?" Sam said. He tossed his towel on a chair and lowered himself into the first warm pool.

I surrendered, casting my own towel to the chair. We sat on a ledge in the pool, a cold drizzle falling on our shoulders. After a few minutes, nudity no longer seemed like a big deal. Without swimsuits, the human body was a neutral thing detached from eroticism, though I still wrapped my towel around myself as we moved from one pool to another. We explored the resort's attractions: the large lukewarm pool, several hotter pools, a small cold pool walled in colorful tile, a sauna and steam room separated by a cedar deck. When we'd completed a full circuit and were back in the first pool, I glanced at the clock above the locker-room entrance and saw that only an hour had passed. My chest tightened, and I wondered if perhaps we had come for too long.

As we sat in the lukewarm pool, I allowed my gaze to alight momentarily on other people. Across from us was an older man with long, stringy gray hair pulled into a ponytail, his eyes closed, his thin lips serenely compressed. Over at the cold plunge, four friends in their twenties took turns dipping their bodies into the frigid water, their mouths opening in muted screams. A couple emerged from the sauna. They seemed oddly matched—the woman was average-looking, in her late thirties, with a soft body and a pinched, unremarkable face, while the man was tall and muscular, with the striking good looks of a young actor.

I nudged Sam. "Do you think he's a blot?" I whispered, nodding toward the couple.

"A what?"

I didn't know how anyone could have missed hearing about blots, as there'd been extensive news coverage of the latest advancements in pirated blot technology. I explained the phenomenon, and Sam nodded, his face set in mild bemusement. I felt agitated by his disinterest. I wanted to provoke more of a reaction.

"When we first started dating, I was worried you might be one," I said.

"Oh yeah?"

"I was on the lookout for clues."

Sam shrugged. "Well, sorry to disappoint you," he said, giving my left thigh a playful squeeze.

The conversation lapsed again. I was annoyed Sam wouldn't join me in speculation over the mismatched couple, who had retreated into the locker room. On the drive up, we'd had music as a buffer, allowing us to pass long stretches without speaking. As we settled in for a last pre-dinner soak in the hottest pool, I waited to see what he would talk about, in the absence of external cues. He began complaining that the resort forbade cooking meat on the property; he was worried about getting enough protein to maintain the muscle mass he'd painstakingly built at the gym. I asked him what he ate during the week, when we were apart, and he said mostly skinless chicken with mixed greens, and vanilla-flavored Muscle Milk.

"Wow," I said. "You're a protein fiend."

Sam gave me a cross look. "I wouldn't say that," he said.

"No?"

"You make it sound stupid."

"That wasn't how I meant it," I said, though I realized it was. I was nervous, eager to lighten the mood. I began telling a story about one of my exes, a younger guy who played bass in a Tool cover band called Stool. I'd met him at a meeting. Before he got sober, he'd spent a year eating only sardines in mustard sauce, which he bought tins of at Safeway on his liquor runs. In his first six months sober, he'd eaten only ice cream, a gallon a day.

"When we dated, though, he was back to a pretty regular diet," I said. "Well, regular enough. He still ate a lot of ice cream."

Sam's mouth was a pink dash set within a tumult of beard growth. "Gross," he said.

"Sure," I said. "He thought so, too."

"I'd rather not hear about other guys you've dated," Sam said.

This caught me off guard. "Why not?"

"Especially if they're weird dudes who eat only sardines."

"That was just one thing about him," I said. "He had a lot of good qualities, too."

"I don't think it's wise to talk about previous partners," Sam said. "You've done that before, and it was a turnoff then, too."

I felt stung by Sam's comment. I watched myself descend into a familiar, sulky silence. Sam tried to cajole me back into a good mood on our walk to the showers. I sensed his desperation when he pointed out a set of ceramic goose planters near the lukewarm pool. "Cute," I agreed, absently.

We rinsed the minerals from our skin and dressed in the locker room. As we walked down the gravel drive to the main lodge, the kitchen in which we'd stashed our meatless groceries, Sam took my hand.

"Are you okay?" he said.

"I'm fine," I said stiffly.

"Hey," Sam said. He stopped and turned to face me. "I'm sorry, okay?"

"It's fine," I said, meeting his gaze. "I won't talk about my exes again."

"No, don't say that," he said. "I want you to talk about whatever you want."

He was smiling hopefully. I could see that he really was sorry, though I suspected he didn't know why he should be.

We hugged, and I resolved to put the incident behind us. I shouldn't have brought up my ex from the Tool cover band. I'd done so in reaction to Sam's protein obsession, which I found off-putting. It was reasonable to not want to hear about a partner's past relationships.

We went inside and made wraps with vegetables and tempeh, stir-fried in a cast-iron skillet. We ate in an adjacent section of the lodge that resembled a train car, tables pushed against windows that overlooked a lush, forested ravine. Though he'd apologized, I still felt distant from Sam, as if something had been left unresolved.

"I'd like you to talk about whatever you want, too," I said.

Sam's jaw clenched in response to this topic. He must have thought he'd escaped. "Okay," he said. "Pretty sure that's what I've been doing."

"I mean, I'd like to hear more about your past," I said. "Your exes, for instance."

Sam laughed. "Why does this feel like therapy all of a sudden?"

"Have you ever done therapy?" I said, perking up at the reference.

Sam's face reddened. "A few times, with my ex. Couples counseling."

"Was it helpful?"

"I dunno," Sam said, unfolding his wrap and picking out chunks of tempeh. "I'm not good at talking about feelings. It's just the way I was raised, I guess."

———

I reminded myself of the importance of accepting a partner exactly as he was in this moment, as I'd advised my friends to do when they came to me with complaints about their relationships. But our first minor conflict had broken a dam of judgment within me. As the second day proceeded, I picked up on additional things Sam did that annoyed me. At one point, we had the sauna to ourselves, and I'd begun telling a story about my friend from college who was having problems in her marriage when Sam emitted a false, barking laugh.

"What's so funny?" I said, startled.

"Nothing," he said. "It's a thing my brother and I do sometimes."

"Are you not interested in what I have to say?"

At that moment, the mismatched couple entered the sauna. The woman draped a towel on the bench below us and lay her body across it, tits up, while the blot-looking man sat in one of the Adirondack chairs, legs spread wide. He met my gaze briefly, his full lips curling into a smile. Save me, I thought.

"It's not like that," Sam said quietly, patting my thigh. "It's just a joke."

Later, as we sat in one of the warm pools, I told Sam about my work at the art school, the long hours of idleness, my feelings of shame and worthlessness as I continued collecting a paycheck for simply existing in a room.

"So you're getting paid to do nothing?" he said. "Sounds pretty great."

I found I couldn't properly convey the absurdity of my role. I probably just sounded spoiled. I switched tack, telling him about the meetings I went to, the recovery program I worked. Sam had been supportive, early on, of my sobriety, saying it was good that I'd "figured my shit out." But as I talked about the beauty of how meetings brought together all types of people, I realized I must sound brainwashed, as though I belonged to a New Age cult. The task of accounting for my life to a stranger filled me with an acute self-loathing. Maybe this was why I'd avoided dating for so long.

I lapsed into silence, feeling judged, though Sam had said nothing. I turned and saw that his eyes were closed, his head tilted back against the edge of the pool. He appeared to be meditating, or maybe he'd fallen asleep.

By the third night, I longed to be back in my apartment, with the cats. At dinner, I nodded through Sam's commentary on the lodge's décor, having given up on planting seeds for a conversation of genuine depth. We had eaten most of the food we'd brought, and were down to wheat tortillas and trail mix. I ate a toasted tortilla, tearing off one small piece at a time and dotting it with Tapatío, while Sam picked nuts out of the trail mix. On the other side of the dining room, the average woman and her hot boyfriend sat, drinking red wine and eating a colorful vegetable stir-fry. I was annoyed that the man had continued existing. I'd been certain he was a blot, and that one night he'd vaporize. I imagined we'd see the woman alone in the pools, making the most of her remaining vacation before heading back to a life rendered chaotic by the blot's aggressions. But here they were still, wearing plush robes and speaking animatedly, in hushed voices. At one point, the woman laughed at something the man had said, then glanced at us guiltily, as if embarrassed to have disrupted the serenity of the lodge.

When we returned to our room, I initiated sex, hoping to work some angle of Sam into myself in a way that would yield pleasure. We moved our bodies quietly, not wanting to disturb the other guests. When it was over we lay in the dark, my head resting on Sam's chest. I had been naked and wet for most of the last three days. My hair was tangled, still damp, smelling of the tea-tree shampoo provided in the communal shower. I had not worn makeup since we arrived. I hadn't looked at a screen since we got here, our phones powered down and locked in my trunk. I'd had every opportunity to be fully present with Sam, but the absence of distraction had only revealed our disconnection. I felt as though my true self were locked in a vault back in the city. I imagined Sam possessed a similar vault, but I was still unable to picture what it might contain.

"It's so nice here," I whispered. Sam didn't know it, but this was my final attempt. I was giving him one last chance to reveal some soft part of himself he'd kept hidden.

But he only murmured, "Mm-hmm." Minutes passed, and I felt his muscles tense and then slacken beneath my arm. The old loneliness washed through me. I thought back to the dinner party where I'd met Roger, the blot. How he had asked me questions with real interest. How he'd noticed when my glass was empty, and taken it upon himself to refill it.

In the morning we drove south on 101, back to the city. I was eager to be rid of Sam. I had mistaken his placid surface for depth, but instead he was like one of the hot springs we'd stewed in all weekend, murky and stagnant, fed from the earth's unknowable core. I asked him to control the music, and I turned the volume up loud, so we wouldn't have to talk.

I told Sam I'd drop him off near the Civic Center BART station. I pulled over on McAllister and put my flashers on. Sam unbuckled his seatbelt, placed his hand on my knee, and gazed into my eyes. Once again, I felt that he was imitating something from a movie. His gestures of affection now seemed parodic, like the false laugh he'd interrupted me with, a joke he shared with his brother, in absentia, at my expense. "Great weekend," he said, and I nodded.

"It really was," I said. Sam cupped the side of my face in his hand—his signature move, I thought bitterly—and planted a long kiss on my mouth. I was relieved when he finally got out of the car. I watched him stand at the corner of McAllister and Polk, waiting for the light to change. From this distance, he could have been anyone, his existence a neutral fact, untethered from mine. It occurred to me that Sam might be a blot after all, a new kind that aimed at a longer-term deception by keeping his host at arm's length. It occurred to me that it didn't really matter either way.

The light changed, and Sam crossed the street and disappeared beyond the stone facade of the library. I was relieved that he didn't turn back and wave.

Back home, the cats journeyed to the door to greet me, less swiftly than they had in their youth. I opened a can of wet food, sliced the pâté down the middle with the tip of a butter knife, and distributed half onto each of two hexagonal black plates set on the floor. I'd had a neighbor come by and feed them while I was away, but he hadn't scooped out the litter boxes, and I cleared them now of the clumps that had gathered. I saw my apartment with fresh eyes, in the harsh light of a day I had not begun there. It was quiet, and in the stillness I could hear time moving forward.

I had spent three months with Sam—not long, but enough that the prospect of starting over seemed exhausting. I imagined breaking up with him, razing what we had just started to build. I would do the same things with a different man, all the milestones, yet again, with someone new. I would peel myself open and unpack my past for his perusal. We would make juice together. I would clean each piece of the juicer carefully, dry it with a dish towel, replace it in the drawer. There would be a period of mutual excitement at the beginning, and then he would tire of me, or I of him. It would last however long it lasted, and then it would end.

From my bag, my phone dinged. Sam had already texted, which surprised me. *Great weekend,* he'd written, in lazy repetition of the sentiment he'd expressed in the car. He punctuated his message with a heart emoji, the first such icon he'd ever sent. I knew he considered this significant, and assumed I would, too, akin to a profession of love.

I lowered myself onto the loveseat. I didn't reply to Sam's text immediately, but I already had an idea of what I would write, and that I might come to regret it.

A week ago, I was walking through Golden Gate Park on my way to the Haight, to have dinner with my friend from college who was now going through a divorce. I passed a clearing where five identical-looking men sat at a picnic table. It was a strange sight, one that made me pause. On further inspection they were not identical; their features were slightly different, though they all possessed the same height and build, and held themselves with the same prim, upright posture. They spoke calmly while playing a card game. I was struck by how comfortable they all seemed with each other, as if they'd been acquainted long enough that they did not have to say much in order to be understood.

Then one of them spotted me. His golden-brown eyes lit up, his energies activated and channeled in my direction. "Hey!" he said, extricating himself from the picnic table and jogging toward me. "You look like a fascinating, intelligent woman, a person with much to offer. Do you want to go on a date? Have you ever witnessed the beauty of Big Sur in the summertime?"

The others turned, eyes flaring, long, perfect hands laying cards on the table.

I moved toward the space they had cleared for me.

The Last Woman on Earth

The Last Woman on Earth lives in Los Angeles. She is single and in her thirties, five foot seven, 145 pounds, a Virgo. She is the world's most famous celebrity. Her talk show has the largest viewership of any TV program, with higher ratings than the Super Bowl and reruns of Miss Universe pageants. The Last Woman on Earth is not particularly talented or charismatic. She blinks a lot and frequently garbles her script from the teleprompter. Prior to the extinction of every other woman, the Last Woman on Earth lived in Ohio and taught preschool. She didn't ask to be the Last Woman on Earth, but she's doing the best she can.

The Last Woman on Earth's talk show is called *Afternoon Programming with the Woman*. She models the show after

Oprah. In the first season, men come on and sit in leather chairs and reminisce about women they used to know. Some men talk about their former wives and girlfriends, but most talk about their mothers. It's like therapy, but the Last Woman on Earth isn't a therapist, so she just sits there and nods and utters validating phrases like "Wow" and "Oh no!" and "That sounds tough." The men always cry. The Last Woman on Earth gets tired of hearing about mothers and in the second season changes the focus of her show to baking.

Five days a week, the Last Woman on Earth bakes a fresh pie in the studio kitchen. She ties her hair in a kerchief and wears a white apron printed with cherries. She invites experts in various fields to come talk to her while she bakes. For forty-five minutes the expert lectures to her sweatered back while she rolls out store-bought dough, mixes fruit with cornstarch, and brushes her lattice crusts with egg wash. A split screen shows a close-up of the pie in progress alongside the face of the expert as he drones on about urban planning or carpentry or neuroscience or poetry. At the end of each episode, the Last Woman on Earth presents the finished pie to the expert. She serves him a piece and waits for him to tell her it's the best pie he's ever had, hands down, bar none, etc.

Thousands of men apply to come on the show. Everyone wants to taste pie made by a woman. When the expert has had his fill of pie, the Last Woman on Earth thanks him and retires to a dimly lit lounge, where she drinks cocktails with a female friend who is played by a mop. The Last Woman on Earth recounts to her friend all the interesting information she learned from the day's expert. Sometimes a production assistant crawls onto the set and gives the mop handle a shake so it looks like the friend is listening. The episode ends whenever the Last Woman on Earth begins weeping, at which point the screen fades to black.

The Last Woman on Earth appears on the cover of every issue of *Us Weekly*. Countless articles discuss her dating life, speculating on why she won't settle down with one of the hundreds of millions of age-appropriate heterosexual men left in the world. In reality the only men who want to date the Last Woman on Earth are perverts and fame-seekers. It's too much pressure, dating the only woman. Normal men would rather just date each other.

In her spare time, the Last Woman on Earth enjoys hiking Runyon Canyon in clumsy male drag and making paintings that depict extinct species: the West African black rhinoceros, the Pyrenean ibex, the Caribbean monk seal. But the Last Woman on Earth's free time dwindles as her empire continues to grow. Her schedule is packed with meetings, with her agent, her personal trainer, foreign heads of state, and her ghostwriter, Phillip, who's hard at work on her memoir, tentatively titled *The Woman Who Wouldn't Die*. Her website receives thousands of inquiries a day. Men turn to her whenever they want a female perspective. Typically they are struggling to interpret the actions of a woman from their past. They turn to the Last Woman on Earth for closure. A team of interns handles this correspondence, typically by sending a form response that emphasizes staying in the present moment by practicing mindfulness.

But as years pass, men are less and less interested in what the Last Woman on Earth has to say. Thought pieces are published on *Slate* and *Medium* with titles like "The Increasing Irrelevance of the Woman." The Last Woman on Earth reads comments on these articles, and on YouTube clips of her show, and on gossip blogs that dissect her nonexistent love life. Many men wish the Last Woman on Earth were better. She's so average, they say. Why couldn't we be left with Rihanna or Megan Fox? Or, if not a physical beauty, at least a woman who's a genius, or one who knows lots of jokes. Men comment that her pies probably aren't that good. She uses recipes from the old Martha Stewart website, and doesn't even make her own dough. One commenter points out that there are thousands of talented male bakers in the world, but none of them gets his own show. Everything she does would be done better by one of earth's numerous men. The Last Woman on Earth agrees with this assessment. She is often sad.

In the seventh season of her talk show, the Last Woman on Earth returns to the *Oprah* format. This time, she invites negative commenters onto the show and allows them to insult her to her face. Most of them are ashamed and say they're sorry, which irritates her because it does not make for good TV. Once in a while she'll get a real fighter who tells her exactly what he thinks of her. The Last Woman on Earth feels truly alive in these moments. She instructs her cameramen to zoom in on her as the man spews his vitriol, capturing the subtle pain that flickers across her stoic face. But the audience hates these episodes. We only have one woman, her supporters point out. We need to treat her right. All the men who criticize her on camera are murdered sooner or later. The Last Woman on Earth is horrified by the violence committed in her name. She goes back to baking pies.

When the Last Woman on Earth dies, days shy of her fortieth birthday, the 405 is shut down for a ten-mile funeral procession that is simulcast worldwide. No one goes to work that day. Everyone watches the funeral of the Last Woman on Earth, in bars and recreation centers and women's restrooms that have been repurposed as shrines commemorating the former existence of women. Men try to outdo each other in performing their grief. They dress up as the Last Woman on Earth, wearing wigs and lipstick and aprons over vintage circle skirts. Privately, they are relieved that the Last Woman on Earth is gone. They can finally do and say whatever they want. The English language is restored to its former simplicity. Everyone speaks freely about the fate of mankind.

It is a golden era for men, those fifty-six years it takes for the human species to die out. The Last Man on Earth is ninety-four years old when he moves to Los Angeles. He broadcasts subversive, thought-provoking, and hilarious skits from the studio where the Last Woman on Earth had once taped her show. He wishes there was someone left to see his show, which is much better than hers was. He should have had his own talk show sixty years ago. Instead, the Last Woman on Earth had been handed a talk show, not because she deserved it, but simply because she was a woman. The Last Man on Earth dies with resentment in his heart.

Heart Seeks Brain

At happy hour, my coworker Sarah and I bond, in the way of women, by cataloguing the flaws of our internal organs. We discover we have a lot in common. Our carotid arteries are of similar diameter, thicker than the feminine ideal. Both our spleens are mildly engorged. We both have always wished our small intestines were a few feet longer, like those of the world's top fashion models. We have longed also for smaller, daintier kidneys. Sarah tells me about her high school rival, Betsy, whose kidneys were the size of a toddler's fists and perfectly shaped. Betsy was the darling of all the renal boys, who in Sarah's school were the cutest.

But Betsy never had anything on my liver, Sarah says. She tells me about her abnormally slender liver, only eight centimeters thick. I am jealous, and say so. In eighth grade I tried to slim my liver to win the affection of Robbie Brookshire, a precocious hepatic fanatic. I consumed nothing but cranberry juice and flaxseed oil for weeks, until I was so malnourished I could hardly get out of bed. It didn't work anyway. The one time we made out, in a Wendy's restroom, Robbie immediately put his hands under my shirt. His fingers pressed beneath my right ribcage, probing until he could feel the lower edge of my liver. He pulled away, disappointed by my liver's breadth, and we avoided each other for the next five years.

But that was junior high, twenty years ago, when many boys were liver-crazy. They were unsophisticated, having barely hit puberty, and were only mimicking the liver mania that was at that time ubiquitous in music videos and the centerfold pages of men's magazines. I play up my jealousy of Sarah's liver because I'm eager to gain her trust. We're sitting at a round metal table outside a boardwalk restaurant a few blocks from our office building. The sun is setting over the ocean and we both have our backs turned to it. I asked Sarah out for drinks because she just started working at our office, and I could use a new friend—a real one, not just a coworker. My female friends have all coupled up with men who are feeding off their organs and whose organs they are feeding off of, a symbiotic process that will continue until they break up or one of them dies. If and when they return to me, single again, they'll be diminished in body and spirit—feet swollen from renal failure, or eyes jaundiced, or breath coming short, a piece of their lung or liver or kidney on a shelf in some man's house.

Sarah tells me it's the same with her friends. They all claim it's worth it to be in a relationship, despite the risk of permanent deformity. I know how it is, Sarah says. You're so relieved to escape a relationship more or less intact, and then you get lonely and jump right back in for another round with someone new. You think, if only you could find a partner whose desire manifests in a relatively noninvasive way. But of course it's a foolish hope. The more someone loves you, the more he'll want to meddle with the most vital parts of you, and vice versa. The only way to not hurt someone is not to love him enough, to remain unmoved by the thought of his organs pulsing beneath a thin layer of skin.

I've never heard it put so well. I nod dumbly and peel open a packet of crackers. I tell Sarah how I'm always on the look-out for a heart man who will appreciate my lopsided ventricles. I thought I found one last week, on a first date with a thickset mathematician who wore unfashionable straight-leg jeans that somehow suggested sexual competence. His eyes flared at the mention of my left ventricle, which is three millimeters longer than the right. I continued, with cautious hope, to detail my circulatory system. My blood is type O. My red blood cells are on the small side, with a diameter of six micrometers. I described my aorta in lurid detail. His mouth had fallen open. Later, in his car, I drew back my hair and allowed him to press his thumbs along my external jugulars, which are unusually pronounced for a woman.

My date, it turned out, was a classic vein man. Sarah rolls her eyes and says vein men are tedious. They all want to be vampires, she says, it's pathetic. I disagree. I've always preferred the attentions of circulatory men. In my view, a vein man is simply a heart man whose development has stalled. Sarah asks if I've heard from the mathematician since our date. I admit he hasn't called yet. Shouldn't have led with the jugulars, she says with a shrug.

The sun has slipped behind the docks. We order a dozen oysters and another bottle of wine. We're quiet while the waiter sets the platter of oysters in front of us. He takes his time arranging the paper napkins and miniature forks. He is young, tall, voluptuously handsome, and he lingers over our table, staring at our abdomens while he lines up our forks and tops off our wine glasses. A gastro man, typically shameless.

Sarah picks up an oyster and dabs it with horseradish. I ask what she's into, and she blushes. I always say I'm into livers, she says, just to see what a guy will do for me. I know he's committed if he'll go under the knife to get me a tissue sample. I've got jars at home in a mini-fridge. It was like a sport in my twenties. Once I had a piece of their liver, I lost interest, I knew I had them. Anyway, my real thing is spines.

She rushes on—I know, I know, and believe me, I wouldn't expect anyone to do it who I wasn't really sure about. I'll spend months feeling a guy out. It's hard to find a partner who's open to the idea of even localized paralysis. That's sort of what the whole liver thing was, like a test of his devotion. If he's not willing to give me a liver sample, there's no way he'll go through lumbar puncture to get me a vial of spinal fluid. And that's only the beginning of what I want from him.

Sarah's words hang in the air. I'm shocked by her cavalier attitude regarding spine kink. I want to choose my words carefully, so as not to offend her. I think it's great you have such a clear idea of what you want in a partner, I say finally.

Our attractive waiter has turned on the heat lamps. When he comes to check on us he forgets himself and asks an awkwardly phrased question: How are your stomachs responding to the oysters?

Fine, Sarah says, shooting him a look meant to contain him. He retreats, humiliated. You can never pick out a gastro man anymore, she says. They used to all be pervy little dweebs in their mom's basement. Now they look like *that*. She sips at her wine, and for a moment I dislike her. Sarah's disdain for the waiter seems hypocritical, given her own extreme tastes.

What about you? she says. What's your thing? I pause, considering whether to give my usual tame answer of kidneys, or tell her the truth. Like Sarah, I'm into the nervous system, but my passion is for the brain itself. My ideal relationship would be with a heart man who possesses a powerful, methodical brain, preferably an expert in some STEM discipline. My dream is that we will marry and he will allow me to take his brain from him, year after year, a tiny bit at a time, through shock treatments and partial lobotomies, until he can't function on his own and I have to care for the drooling husk of his body until it expires. It is only for this that I'd surrender pieces of my literal heart.

In my whole life I've told only a few people about this desire; brain play remains the ultimate taboo. A person can function with three quarters of a liver, a lung trimmed at the edges, a few punctured veins. But once you fuck with the brain, consent becomes an issue. Sarah waits for my answer. I know she doesn't really care about me, doesn't find me interesting. If anything, she might use my deviance against me in the future, when we are both vying for promotion. So I tell her I'm into kidneys, and she shrugs and says, popular choice.

The waiter brings our check. On my way out I slip him my number. We meet under the boardwalk when his shift is over. We lie on the sand and he pulls out a stethoscope, running its cold diaphragm over my abdomen. He listens to the oysters and crackers and wine work their way through my digestive tract. This is the furthest I'll let him go. A gastro man is lucky for what he can get, even if he's young and gorgeous, and the waiter seems to know this. I stare at the moon and imagine it looks down on my love, the human casing of the brain I have dreamed of ever since I was a girl crouched behind the refrigerator door, fondling heads of cauliflower without knowing why.

The Void Wife

lise planned to enter the void alone. She didn't want to
be anyone's void wife, and certainly not Robert's.

Unfortunately, Robert wasn't taking no for an answer.
On the day the void was scheduled to hit San Francisco, Elise
snuck away from the camp they'd made on Ocean Beach with
other void refugees. She hid from him in the ruins of the
Sutro Baths, gazing out at the Pacific while behind her, Oakland was negated.

The void had appeared six months ago in a slender belt
around the globe near the 90th meridian, slicing through
Dubuque and Guatemala, Bhutan and the Kirov Islands of
Russia. Since then it had expanded in both directions at the
rate of seventy miles a day, like two immense lids drawing
over the eye of the earth.

In Kansas City, Elise and her boyfriend, Dave, had watched groups of people holding hands as they hurled themselves against the veil. Their silhouettes, limbs outstretched, remained outlined for a few seconds before fading to black. Everyone believed that the void was a portal to an unspoiled earth. Everyone also believed you'd exist for eternity with the people you were touching at the moment of absorption. Elise held out against this idiocy. Death was just death, same as always.

Now Elise wished she'd voided herself with Dave when she had the chance. At 4:00 P.M. the cruise ship Robert had commandeered would push back from Pier 31. The ship would churn through the San Francisco Bay and pass beneath the Golden Gate Bridge before setting sail on the Pacific. Its passengers would enjoy a few additional months of existence at sea until the margins of void closed around them. Elise knew she should crawl into a sea cave and wait for the void to take her alone. If she was wrong, and there was an eternity, she couldn't risk being stuck there with Robert.

But Elise was a coward. Elise loved existence. She rushed back to camp, where Robert was packing the Prius.

"Cutting it close!" he said, kissing both her cheeks. He was still somehow wearing cologne.

After their Kansas City apartment was absorbed by the void, Elise and Dave had driven west to collect their parents. The first stop was Oklahoma, where Elise's mother and father lived in a replica of her childhood home. Tornadoes had leveled the ranch house once when she was twelve and again when she was in college. Her parents rebuilt each time, with slightly less care than before. Elise stood in the living room, making note of the canted ceiling, the rough margins of carpet, the unpainted drywall.

"We've stayed put through worse storms," Elise's mom said.

"It's not a tornado, Mom. It's a curtain of absence that negates everything it touches."

"Might as well be negated in our own house, then."

"You kids can come with us, if you want," Elise's dad said. Her parents were sitting on the couch, her mom's legs draped over her dad's lap. They were ready.

The wall behind the couch began to dim. Elise grabbed her mom's bony wrists and tried to wrench her from the couch, but her mom shook her off and slapped her face.

"Get on, then, if you're so keen on existing," her mom said. It was true: Elise was keen on existing, if only for a few more months. She'd imagined driving cross-country with her parents like they had when she was a kid, processing a few last things together before the end. But it was clear that her parents were already lost.

Elise and Dave stood on the sidewalk and watched the house be eaten away in pixels of void. They got back in the car only when it was certain that her parents no longer existed, unable to change their minds and come along, even with perhaps a voided-out smeary stump where an arm or leg had been. Elise cried quietly, staring into the side mirror at the satiny black wall.

"It's okay," Dave said. "They have each other in eternity."

"You believe in that crap now?"

He shrugged. "I don't *not* believe in it."

"I thought you were an atheist."

Dave said that God had nothing to do with it.

The next day they rolled into Colorado Springs, where Dave's dad lived in a large condominium complex. They sat with him by the pool, which was clotted with children. School had been called off due to the encroaching void. It was 11:00 A.M. and already hot. Drops of sweat fell from Dave's dad's chin into the joint he was rolling.

Dave begged his dad to come with them.

"Sometimes you just gotta cash in your chips," Dave's dad said. A woman in her fifties, wearing heavy makeup and a tall lacquered hairdo, brought over a crystal bowl of fruit salad. She put her hand on the meaty shoulder of Dave's dad and glared over it.

"Fruit salad," the woman said. It did not seem like an offer. Elise guessed that Dave's dad had taken this woman as his void wife, and she didn't want children from his first marriage joining them in eternity.

Dave cried as he hugged his dad goodbye.

His dad shrugged. "Why're you crying? You know that void's a straight chute to heaven."

In the car, Dave said he was kind of glad his dad refused to come, because that meant his mom would be more likely to join them.

"I know it's terrible, but if I had to lose one parent to the void it would definitely be my dad."

" 'Straight chute to heaven,' " Elise said. "Must be nice to buy into that fairy tale."

"Maybe he's right, Elise," Dave said, irritated. "Wouldn't you rather think that your parents are in heaven right now?"

Elise's tears resurged upon mention of her voided parents. Dave muttered an apology and handed her a Subway napkin from the sheaf in his door pocket.

Dave's mom lived in the Rockies with her boyfriend, Stuart, a geologist. The back of their cabin jutted over a chasm. The four of them sat in Adirondack chairs on the deck and looked at the mountains. Behind them, the sun was setting, bloodying the snow-capped peaks.

"We can't wait to watch the mountains get voided," Dave's mom said.

"I've spent my whole career studying those damn rocks," Stuart said. "It's going to be a relief."

Dave drew Elise into the kitchen.

"Maybe we should stay here," he said. "Stuart seems like an interesting guy to spend eternity with."

Elise had had enough. "There is no eternity!" she said. "The void is the void. Anything else is a fantasy. What's happened to you?"

"You don't know that for sure," Dave said. "What if you're wrong? You really want it to be just you and me, forever?"

Elise's heart broke a little. Dave wouldn't even commit to a theoretical eternity with her unless his mom and Stuart came along. They'd been together three years, and when the void was first publicized she'd taken for granted that they'd cling to existence together until the bitter end. She hadn't counted on Dave falling for this hype about an afterlife.

Whether the void took them today or four months from now, it was clear they were no longer compatible.

Elise insisted they get back on the road, and Dave reluctantly agreed. They stopped for the night at a motel in Utah. In the morning Dave and his Kia were gone. On the TV screen Elise found a neon green Post-it note with a heart penciled on it. She figured he'd driven back to Colorado, to be voided with his mom and Stuart, or perhaps with his dad and the fruit salad lady. It was for the best, Elise told herself. She hitched her way west until she hit ocean.

At Ocean Beach, the western limit of San Francisco, she found a camp of around a hundred people living in tents. She set her bags in the sand, near a family with two young children who observed her warily. That first night, she met Robert. He'd come to the bonfire with a basket of groceries looted from Safeway. He watched as she warmed a piece of Wonder Bread near the flame. All the good bread had already been looted.

"You're the last babe on the West Coast," he whispered into her ear. She wanted to protest that this couldn't possibly be true. Robert was just terrified of facing the void alone.

Robert had lied about the ship. He wasn't the captain, just another passenger with a cheap interior room. Still, he had saved her. Tickets were scarce, and as they entered the bay Elise gazed at the shore, from which throngs of people begged to be allowed on board. Robert put his arm around her shoulders and coaxed her into their cramped quarters. Elise's first instinct was to shove him away, but she took a deep breath and endured. She planned to lull Robert into complacency so she could escape him at the final moment. Though she maintained that the void led to ordinary death, the propaganda must have seeped into her consciousness on some level. She would allow no part of her body to touch Robert's at the moment of absorption, just in case.

Later that night, the void hit the ocean, which really fucked with the waves. The ship pitched and rolled. Elise allowed Robert to put his tongue in her mouth. The ship heaved again and her jaw closed on the tip of his tongue.

"Ow, Elise," Robert said. "What the fuck?" His tongue was bleeding. She brought him ice chips from the hall.

"Sorry," she said. When he asked if she wanted to hear him play a few new songs on his guitar, she felt she couldn't say no. Robert stared into her eyes as he strummed the guitar and sang in the style of Bob Dylan. She was sure it was a joke, but then he played several more songs and she realized it wasn't. Just a few more months of this, she told herself, and you'll be free.

The last months of existence were terrifying, the ship tossed like a toy as billions of gallons of seawater gushed into the void. In January, the western wall of the void loomed before them, trapping them between the two black margins. It was light for an hour a day, then half an hour, less, as the void closed the sky. The captain steered south, traversing the narrowing channel of sea.

Robert had grafted himself to Elise's side. In the final minutes Elise remarked that they should probably use the bathroom before being voided, just in case it was a long trip.

"Good idea," Robert said. "You stay put, beautiful." The

moment the bathroom door slid shut behind him, Elise ran out of the room, down two flights of stairs to the spa, where she climbed into a hot tub with three women who were wearing blindfolds and earplugs and pressing their fingers into each other's forearms.

Suddenly the ship was still, cradled by the void's walls. Blackness pressed in from both directions. Elise heard Robert's voice calling her name from across the deck. She dipped her head underwater, hoping her air would last long enough. But the void was too slow. She came gasping to the surface, and Robert spotted her. "Elise!" he said. "Thank God!" He jumped into the tub and placed his hands on her knees. The void had begun eating her right and left sides in perfect symmetry and she could no longer move. In her last moments of corporeal existence, just before she was transported to an infinite white plain upon which it was impossible to hide from the orb of bluish light representing Robert, she took small pleasure in watching his face disappear.

Shelter

I n the basement of the house in Iowa that Reese and Mark were renting for the summer, there was a concrete vault, eight by five feet, presumably built as a storm shelter. Reese stored the house's Shop-Vac there, along with a crate of Carr's rosemary crackers she'd drunkenly ordered one night, and a case of wine shipped from their friends' vineyard in Sonoma. Beyond the shelter, in the half-aboveground section of basement, the walls around a window had started to leak. This summer was set to break rainfall records. The threat of catastrophic flooding was on everyone's lips. "Stay dry," strangers told Reese, at the grocery store and the gas station. Rain wept into the pens where the house's owner had once raised rabbits for meat. Each morning, Reese went downstairs, wheeled the Shop-Vac from the shelter, and used it to suck up the night's accumulated water. She resented being left alone with this burden. Mark was always at the studio in Solon, with his band. He was not taking the situation seriously enough.

One day Reese came down to find the door of the shelter locked. It was a metal door with a keyhole in the knob. Reese wrapped her hand around the knob and twisted. She pressed her cheek against the door and listened. She could not quite bring herself to knock.

Reese circled back to the flooded room. Drops of water raced down the wall above the rabbit pens, which still held clay food dishes and a rotting bale of alfalfa, chicken wire threaded with white fur. More rain was forecast for the rest of the week.

Upstairs, Mark stood at the kitchen counter spreading almond butter on toast. From across the kitchen Reese was struck by a vision of him as a stranger. Mark was suddenly not her boyfriend of five years but an unfamiliar man in his late thirties with thinning hair, a swollen stomach, and small, soft hands. She could not imagine spotting this man across a train platform in some Central European capital and allowing the crowd to carry her to him, brushing against him in hope that some part of her would stick, burr-like, to the weft of his flannel.

He turned. The spell broke and Mark was Mark again.

"Did you lock the shelter?" Reese said.

"Huh?"

"The door of the shelter is locked."

"We don't even have a key to that room," Mark said. He shoved the bread back into its sweaty bag. A tuft of almond butter rose from his thumb knuckle. In earlier eras she would have licked it off. It would have launched an erotic exchange.

"The Shop-Vac's locked in the shelter," Reese said. She handed Mark a paper towel. "It's getting wet down there."

"I'll call a contractor today. This guy Todd Fischer has good Yelp reviews."

"I don't like the name Todd." Reese had had an unsettling sexual encounter with a Todd in high school, in the wings of the stage where the marching band practiced. During their courtship Mark would have seized upon this allusion, a thread he could pull to unravel her.

Mark peeled his jacket from the back of a chair. "I'm late. See you tonight." He kissed her cheek, hurting her with his beard.

They'd come to Iowa so Mark and his psychedelic metal band, Psilocybin, could finish their new album. Eight months ago, Reese and Mark had received a no-fault eviction notice from their apartment in San Francisco. Their landlord was selling the building to condo developers. Mark and Reese accepted the legally mandated thirty-thousand-dollar relocation payment. They complained bitterly on social media but were secretly relieved to be thrust from the city. Most of their friends had already moved to LA or Portland.

Reese kept her job as a copywriter for a pornographic website that catered to certain increasingly mainstream kinks that fell under the rubric of BDSM. She was tasked with crafting unique descriptions for videos that had all begun to merge together in what she imagined as a vat of yowling, flesh-toned putty. The day she found the shelter locked, Reese sat at the kitchen table with the jar of almond butter and a spoon. She logged in to her work email and unzipped the folder with the day's batch of videos. In the first, a naked girl with very pale skin had been rigged to an erotic torture device in the company's cavernous brick-lined studio. The girl was blindfolded, her back fixed in an extreme arch. A bald, oiled man entered the room and began to lap at her vagina. The girl shrieked with pleasure, though the man's technique was questionable. After a few minutes he left. Two women wearing latex body suits entered the room and began inserting dildos of escalating girth into the girl's asshole.

Reese fast-forwarded, searching for elements she'd need to mention in her description. She jotted notes on a legal pad. Right on cue, at the twenty-one-minute mark, the bald man reappeared and masturbated until his semen latticed the girl's wide, youthful face. Reese thought of cinnamon buns. Her stomach growled; she spooned almond butter into her stale mouth. On the pad she wrote "Facial."

After three hours Reese had written descriptions for five videos. She snapped her laptop closed, stood and stretched, peeled a freckled banana. Mark had texted, *Todd coming tomorrow. Sorry his name is Todd.*

Reese walked to the sliding door, pried the dowel from its gutter, and stepped into the thick air of the screened-in deck. Drizzle perforated the sodden lawn. Insects moaned. Heat gathered on her skin like a shroud.

For the first few weeks, Reese had enjoyed the solitude of her days, the big windows opening onto the creek and blurry hills that comprised their glut of land. Now she felt uneasy.

The house had locked its inner chamber against her. It was rejecting her as a body rejects a foreign object: a silicone implant, a valve from the heart of a pig. She wished Mark hadn't taken the car to the studio that morning, though she did not know where she would go if she had it.

The afternoon held three fucking-machine videos, two dungeon orgies, and one caning tutorial. When she'd finished her synopses Reese transferred a load of laundry to the dryer and went to the basement to check on the water level. She held her hand under the sill and let rain drip into her palm. She brought her cupped hand to her face and dipped her tongue in. The water tasted like metal and cut grass and the dryer sheet she'd just held.

Reese knew she had to drain the pool on the floor before the mold issued poison through the vents. She went to the shelter and twisted the knob again. She leaned her weight against the door. She kicked its white face, the sole of her Vans leaving a feathered gray scuff.

The house's owner, Scott, was a friend of Mark's parents. He had lived in Shanghai for a decade with his Chinese wife and their son. Reese went upstairs, closed the porn tabs on her browser, and began composing an email to Scott. Mark would not like her doing this. He would want to parse her email for tact before she sent it, because Scott was letting them live there for almost nothing. But Reese was annoyed at how unhelpful Scott had been regarding the basement leak. He'd told them to have it fixed, and that he'd reimburse them, but how were they supposed to know who to hire, who would give them a fair price? Now there was the matter of this shelter for which they had no key. *I look forward to your prompt attention regarding this matter*, she concluded.

Reese struggled to individuate her descriptions of the three fucking-machine videos. She was running out of ways to describe a vagina as hungry. *Her pussy is ravenous. Her pussy had a light lunch and now it's dinnertime. Her pussy slavers for nourishment. Her pussy is about to faint from low blood sugar. Her pussy carries almonds in its purse to tide it over until the next meal.*

An email pinged in her box. Hairs rose on Reese's forearms, her constituent cells priming for battle. *Sorry, but I'm not sure what you mean*, Scott had written. *That room locks from the inside.*

Mark brought home a rotisserie chicken from the Solon supermarket. They sat at the kitchen table and ate the chicken along with a salad Reese had made from what was left in the crisper: heirloom tomatoes with the bruises cut out, a rubbery yellow pepper, slivered red onion, and a conspicuously large, wrinkled cucumber reduced to harmless cubes.

"Water's getting deep down there," Reese said.

"Todd's coming tomorrow," Mark said. "He can check out the lock, too."

"Can you take the day off? I don't want to be alone in the house with a stranger."

"I would, but we've really gotta keep plugging away on these last tracks," Mark said. "Todd's a solid dude. Nothing but five stars on Yelp."

Reese watched as Mark tore the skin from a breast and set it aside. He pried up shards of white meat with his fork and wrapped the meat in its own skin, then placed the packet in his mouth so the skin wouldn't lodge between his incisors. He appeared so self-possessed, so contented by his tiny rituals, that Reese was filled with resentment. She knew her anger didn't correspond to the actual structure of their lives. She was free to do as she liked. She was not bound to the home by anything but the fact that they possessed a single car. And yet she felt a primordial rage toward Mark, as though he were a brute husband who went out to conquer the world, while she was trapped in this house with its flooded basement. She endeavored to say nothing to Mark, and to observe how much time would pass before he noticed.

Reese waited while Mark washed the grease from his hands in the kitchen sink. When it was her turn, Mark stood behind her and coiled warm, wet fingers around the roots of her hair. He slid his other hand down the front of her sweatpants. She felt his penis firm against her ass. He pulled down her pants and entered her. She came quickly, her orgasm urged along by frustration, her hands planted on the metal floor of the sink.

Mark pulled out and came on the small of her back. Reese stayed still while he blotted the tip of his penis on her tailbone. She waited, bent over the sink, while Mark wetted a dish towel and wiped her down. Reese felt like an expensive horse or a sports car kept under drop cloths and buffed weekly with chamois. Her eyes rested on the surface of the trash, a litter of small gray bones.

"Are you okay?" She looked up and found Mark watching

her carefully, having perceived the threat of her mood. He'd passed the test this time. Her resentment dissolved, and she felt embarrassed for her childishness.

"I'm fine," she said, and leaned over to kiss his cheek above the beard line.

Todd arrived at one the next afternoon. He was a tall, broad-shouldered man in his forties, his hair close-cropped around a deeply corrugated forehead. He looked uncannily similar to a guy from one of the Men in Pain videos Reese had synopsized that morning. In the video the man was tied to a chair with a length of nautical-looking rope. A woman in a red latex bodysuit and six-inch red heels entered the room and made a short speech before flogging him. Reese imagined the performers drinking beer in the Armory Club after the shoot, the woman cracking jokes as she rubbed balm into the man's stiletto welts.

In Todd's presence, Reese folded herself into a hostess persona she had culled from movies and snippets of conventional pornography. She wished she had lemonade to offer.

"Can I get you anything?" she said. "Glass of water?"

Todd said no thanks. "Let's have a look at the issue," he prompted. Reese felt hurt, absurdly, that he cared only about the "issue" and not about her. She realized she'd harbored a fantasy about this working man whom Mark, oblivious to the threat of being cuckolded, had hired and sent to the house to be greeted by his bored girlfriend. She had imagined having to dodge Todd's advances, or perhaps acquiesce to them, depending on how attractive he turned out to be.

But the real Todd was all business. Reese led him down

the basement stairs, wishing she'd worn pants that more aggressively displayed her ass.

Todd stepped into the pool of water. He ran his thumb along the seal of the window, laid his palm on the weeping wall. Reese felt embarrassed, as if it were her own body that was leaking, her salty runoff beneath Todd's thumb. Maybe she was no longer hot. She had wasted her best years on Mark.

"You've got serious groundwater problems," Todd said. "The foundation needs shoring up, but we have to wait for the rain to quit. In the meantime you'll need to keep it as dry as you can. You got a Shop-Vac?"

Reese explained that the Shop-Vac was imprisoned. She led Todd to the shelter. He jiggled the knob, then ran his hands along the edges of the door as if searching for a hidden release.

"The owner says it locks from the inside," she said. "I think somebody's living in there."

She'd been half-joking, but Todd fixed her with a serious look and said, "I highly doubt that." He gave the knob one last turn, then shrugged and said he could at least get the water up. He brought his own Shop-Vac down from his truck. Reese watched the hose suck water into the machine's belly. When he had drained the pool, Todd emptied the Shop-Vac in the utility sink, brushed his hands on his jeans, and said he should be going. Reese flinched at the prospect of his departure, which felt like a rejection. She fumbled for an excuse to make him stay.

"That shelter freaks me out," she said. "Isn't it weird, that it only locks from inside?"

"I'll get my buddy Jake to come by," Todd said. "He's a

lock guy." He carried his Shop-Vac upstairs. Reese followed, observing the shift of his flat ass under faded denim.

"I like the sound of a lock guy," she said, a bit desperately.

"He's a real lock wizard." They stood in the foyer. Reese felt Todd's bulk receding from her grasp. In another moment he would be gone, and she'd be alone with the dripping walls, the locked shelter, and a daunting backlog of Wired Pussy videos.

"What do I owe you?" she said.

"Consultation's free. Call me when it dries up."

He stood in the doorway, waiting for her to release him.

"Are you sure you don't want a glass of water?"

That night, Reese summarized Todd's findings to Mark while he was in the shower.

"So that's good," he said. "We just have to wait for it to dry up."

"He said we have groundwater problems," she said. "We need a new Shop-Vac."

"Don't we have one?"

Reese was so frustrated she wanted to scream. "It's locked in the shelter," she said. "Remember?"

"The lock guy's coming tomorrow, right?"

"Who knows if he'll be able to do anything," Reese said, in a fatalistic tone. She wandered out of the bathroom and lay on the bed. She could hear Mark saying something, thinking she was still in the room, though if he'd simply glanced through the rain glass of the shower door he would have seen she was gone. It was only 7:00 P.M., but she rolled onto her side and pretended to have fallen asleep.

Rain continued through the night. In the morning, the plasterboard above the rabbit pens appeared tender and moist. The pool had deepened to six inches at the corner. Reese imagined plunging her face into the murky water.

She returned to the living room, where she spent the morning summarizing videos in the categories of Water Bondage, Sadistic Rope, Electro Sluts. Her descriptions read increasingly like recipes. *We start her on her back and stuff her until she squirts her savory juices. We finish her standing and drizzled with cream.*

The lock wizard, Jake, arrived at noon. He was slight and hollow-cheeked, sporting a russet mustache. Like Todd, he eschewed small talk and offers of ice water. Reese felt hardened by Todd's dismissiveness the day before, and didn't bother courting Jake's attention. She led him straight to the basement. He crouched under the doorknob of the shelter.

"The owner said the door only locks from inside," Reese said.

"This is a tornado shelter, for sure," Jake said. He caressed the underside of the handle as if it were a woman's breast. Reese's crotch swelled with heat in her tight-fitting jeans.

"He's in Shanghai. The owner. Can't be bothered."

"This door doesn't lock from inside only. If it did, there wouldn't be a real keyhole on the outside. Just a plain round hole."

"I was wondering if someone locked themselves in there."

"You know what," Jake said, standing up. "It's not even locked. The knob must've broke." They were the same height. Jake stared at her lips for a distended moment. Reese held her breath, anticipating contact. Then he twitched and rubbed his cheek on his shoulder.

"I'd been going in and out of there all the time," Reese said. "It's where I keep the Shop-Vac."

"You must've broken it accidentally."

"I don't have that kind of strength."

"If there's someone inside," Jake said, "they can't get out, either."

Reese followed Jake up the steps. He was already halfway through the door. She fought an urge to clutch at the back of his T-shirt. This impulse confused her. Jake was even less attractive than Todd had been, yet she suspected that if he simply asked, she would fuck him right there in the foyer.

"What do I owe you?" she said.

Jake paused on the stoop. He laughed. "I didn't do shit," he said, and was gone.

Psilocybin was running up against the deadline they'd set for the new album. Reese had driven Mark to the studio in the morning, saying she'd come by later with dinner. At 6:00 P.M. she got into the rusted Honda and drove to the supermarket on Main Street, a few storefronts down from the feed store the band had repurposed as a studio. She grabbed a cart and threw in chips and salsa, a twelve-pack of High Life, and a fifth of Jim Beam, then continued to the deli counter. A teenage employee snuck glances at her breasts while depositing meatloaf and slaw into Styrofoam shells. Reese wore a thin sundress under her open rain jacket. She had put on makeup for the first time in weeks, and now wondered why she'd bothered.

"Anything else, miss?" the boy said.

Reese wasn't ready to relinquish his attention. She asked the boy what his favorite deli item was.

"Fried chicken, for sure," he said. He grinned. His teeth were small and crowded. It looked like he had more teeth than usual.

"That's okay."

"Hey, do you know those guys in the band?"

"Yeah. I'm here with them." Reese found herself reluctant to tell him that the guitarist was her boyfriend. She wanted this sixteen-year-old to continue thinking about fucking her, to believe that fucking her was a possibility, however remote. She knew this made her a pervert. She zipped up her jacket.

"Are they a rock band, or what?"

Reese considered explaining Psilocybin's disparate influences, which she figured would impress and baffle the boy. She decided she didn't have the energy. "Sort of," she said.

"Cool," he said, seeming disappointed. He began wiping down the cutting shelf. Reese drifted toward the registers, behind which teenage girls from the Mennonite community perched on wooden stools. They were big-boned and milk-skinned and wore starched dresses, their expertly braided hair concealed under pleated caps.

"Twenty seventy-five," the girl said. Reese swiped her card, glancing with longing at the girl's soft upper arms.

Reese entered the dusty front room of the old feed store. She arranged the food containers and plastic cutlery on the broad pine table and settled in to wait for the band to finish their session. The shelves still held slumped bags of dry goods and decades-old cans of beans and potted meat. Gerald and Eric were living here—Gerald in the meat locker, Eric in the attic. The band initially hoped to set up their studio in the house, but Reese vetoed that plan, saying she needed silence to work. Now she wondered if it would have been better to have them around, the drone of Psilocybin lending her empty days a certain texture.

She cracked a beer and watched lightning flare against the drawn blinds. Thunder sounded in the distance, a prolonged, gastric rumbling. Psilocybin's muddy instrumentals leached through the jury-rigged acoustical foam. In a few minutes the song oozed to silence and the band members emerged from the studio. They dug into the beer and chips. They flipped open the Styrofoam shells with casual brutality. Eric started rolling a blunt. Gerald popped open a bottle of the cold-pressed juice he had delivered from Brooklyn every week. Mark sat beside Reese. He placed his right hand on her thigh. He pinched her quadriceps between thumb and forefinger as if appraising an item he'd forgotten he owned.

"How'd it go with the lock guy?" he said.

Reese explained that the handle was not locked, but broken. While she talked, Gerald thumbed through his Instagram feed. Eric continued crafting the blunt. Mark's eyes glazed and Reese knew he was still thinking about the album. She was annoyed by her own preoccupation with the shelter. Since coming to Iowa, she had begun to embody the role of bored housewife, eager to unpack the minutiae of her lonesome day to whoever would listen.

"He said if someone is in there, they can't get out," she said. Gerald looked up from his phone and squinted, struggling to fill in the parts of her story he hadn't listened to. "The tornado shelter," Reese prompted. "The door handle's broken."

"Weird," Gerald said, and sank back into his phone.

"You must have broken it when you were getting the Shop-Vac out," Mark said.

"Why does everyone think I'm strong enough to break a door handle without realizing it?" Reese said. "I can't do one push-up."

"So you think someone's living in there?" Eric said. He sparked the blunt. "That's tight."

"No one's in there," Mark said.

"If they are, they're dead by now," Reese said. "It's been a week."

"You'll start to notice a smell," Gerald said.

"The smell wouldn't get out. The door is sealed with rubber."

"That's ridiculous," Mark said. "No one's in there, sweetie. The handle just broke somehow."

Eric passed Reese the blunt. She filled her lungs with thick, sweet smoke. Mark asked her to listen to the tracks they'd just recorded and tell them if the sound was sludgy enough.

Reese drank four beers, hoping to forget about the shelter, but instead she just grew angrier at Mark for abandoning her to deal with it. She hoped they'd discover a corpse in the shelter after all, just to shake Mark from his complacency. On the drive home she announced that she was going to break down the door.

"Don't do that," Mark said. "We'll be on the hook for repairs."

"I can't be in the house all day with a dead body rotting under me."

"Come on, sweetie. I know you don't really believe that."

"Who knows? Someone could sneak into the basement in the middle of the night and we wouldn't hear it."

"You know, I think I remember breaking the doorknob," Mark said.

"You do not."

"Yes, I do. I mean, it's definitely a possibility. I was pretty sleep-deprived the last time I used the Shop-Vac."

Reese glared at Mark. "That's such a lie. You always do this."

"Do what?"

"Lie to placate me. To shut me up."

"I don't know what you're talking about, babe."

She realized this was probably true. She'd never known Mark to lie deliberately. He simply believed whatever was convenient to him in the moment, because he was lazy.

Hot air poured from the vents, searing her eyes and throat. "Stop the car," Reese said.

"What?"

"I want to get out."

"We're almost home."

"I'm getting out."

She unbuckled her seatbelt and opened the door. Mark cursed and pulled onto the gravel shoulder. Thunder tore the sky. Lightning revealed a mottled underbelly of cloud. Mark eased the car behind Reese. The rain soaked her clothes, making her heavier with each step. She tilted her face to the rain like a supplicant.

Headlights appeared on the horizon. The sight of them sobered Reese. She worried what the people in the oncoming car would think. She got back into the Honda.

Mark was silent until they pulled into the garage. He opened his door, then paused. "You need to pull yourself together, Reese. This behavior is unacceptable." He went inside. Reese sat in the hot garage for half an hour. She felt a little embarrassed, but also calm, as if a wound had been cauterized.

The morning was clear and warm and windless. Reese went downstairs to find the pond had grown to cover the length of the old rabbit pens. She lingered next to the water heater, the furnace, the throbbing guts of the house. She stood beside a rust-gummed drain, over which she imagined Scott had slit his rabbits' throats.

Mark was already at the studio. He had left without waking her, without bothering to ask if she wanted the car. Reese felt gratified that he was finally taking her seriously enough to be angry at her, but she was also ashamed of how she'd behaved. Mark was easygoing to a fault, able to ride out all but the worst of her moods. He'd acted cold toward her only a handful of times in the course of their relationship, and on those occasions, Reese was frantic to regain his affection, fearing she might have finally lost it for good.

She paused before the door of the shelter. Her blood surged with daring. She knocked on the door. "Hello? Is someone in there?" she said. Above her, a moth ticked its fragile body against a bulb.

Reese began kicking. She kicked as high as she could, attempting to strike every inch of the door's surface, as one might cover a lover's chest in kisses. She kicked until her breath shortened, until her joints ached and the face of the door was dingy with marks, at which point she collapsed on the painted concrete. Reese reflected. Maybe she'd broken the handle after all. Maybe it had been on the verge of breaking, and she'd pulled it too roughly, and something had clicked out of place, for good. When they'd first moved in, she had considered working in the shelter. The door handle could have broken while she was inside. She would have eaten the crackers, drunk the wine, urinated in a corner. Mark would have been forced to hire a man with the proper tools to free her.

Back upstairs, Reese could still feel the filthy water in the basement, as though it were her own untenable foundation, her own loose and watery bowels. She felt the shelter locked beneath her, a diamond-hard kernel of contempt. A parallel version of herself trapped inside, clawing the concrete walls until her fingernails broke off.

Mark arrived home with Thai takeout from the college town twenty miles south, an unambiguous peace offering that flooded Reese with relief. They embraced in the foyer. Reese apologized, explaining how she'd been losing it a little, being alone in the house all day, though of course that wasn't his fault, she had agreed to come here, but she hadn't known what it would be like, not really. She'd lived in cities her whole life, not like Mark, who'd grown up near here. He had often described the idyll of his youth, vignettes involving cruelties to lesser fauna: trapping lightning bugs in Mason jars, tying kite string to the necks of crawfish and leading them like tiny, brittle dogs along the banks of the creek that ran behind his parents' house.

They spread a beach towel on the living room carpet and ate from the takeout cartons with plastic forks. Mark apologized for neglecting Reese, for stranding her at the house. Psilocybin had set a new deadline for the album, which had run into some snags in the mixing process and would need to be remastered. After that they could leave, take a break, go visit friends in New York. But they hadn't really talked about what they would do after the summer, had they? Scott liked having them there, and the rent was absurdly cheap. As he talked, Reese withdrew deeper into herself, nodding numbly at the plans Mark was making for both of them.

They gathered the diminished cartons in a plastic bag, clearing space on the beach towel for make-up sex. Reese moved her limbs in a mechanical dance. She focused on her joints, imagining bones turning in the sockets of other bones, rattling at the ends of strings.

Each morning, Reese descended the stairs and stood at the door of the shelter. She turned the knob. She knocked and pleaded. "Come on, enough of this," she said, in the firm voice she'd once used to extract her younger sister from the bathroom when they were getting ready for school. Around Mark, she concealed her fixation behind a mask of radical compliance. She alluded to staying here through winter.

They would learn the practical skills of their forebears. They would homestead, as Mark had long fantasized. How wonderful, she said moonily, to make their own jams, to lie together in front of the wood-burning stove and read to each other from books of romantic poetry. To knit scarves of virgin wool and plait her hair into braids.

August commenced. The rain was done, the days now relentlessly hot and cloudless. The basement pond had begun to fester and take on a septic smell. On a Thursday, Reese rented a Shop-Vac at Home Depot. As she wheeled it past the door of the shelter, she imagined the Shop-Vacs spoke to each other in their language, the free Vac offering words of condolence and urging fortitude to the one that was imprisoned.

She siphoned the fetid reservoir into the belly of the rented machine. When the ground was dry she felt powerful and light. She called Todd to ask about fixing the house's foundation. He came over the same day and inspected the walls, this time with enthusiasm, making notes on a clipboard. He emailed her an estimate, which she forwarded to Scott, who gave the go-ahead. Work would begin Monday.

Reese gushed about the seamlessness of the process to Mark over dinner.

"I knew you could handle it, sweetie," he said, beaming.

Reese prepared a pitcher of iced tea and a plate of cornbread for Todd and his crew of college-age boys, friends of Todd's son who were home for the summer. Todd anticipated that it would take three days to bolster the failing wall. On the first afternoon, Reese sat in the living room, soothed by the pounding and drilling below her as she synopsized a triptych of gangbang videos.

The men departed at five. Their tools cluttered the rabbit pens. Reese had driven Mark to the studio that morning, and he'd be texting soon for a ride home. She would need to work quickly.

At the side of the shelter, the temple of the shelter's skull, there was a rack of clothes, old suit coats and sequined dresses wrapped in plastic garment bags. A few days before, Reese had gathered these clothes in her arms and set them aside, exposing a plain of drywall. This would be her point of access to the shelter. During breaks from her work, she had watched poorly produced YouTube videos in which paunchy middle-aged men exulted in laying waste to the interior walls of their own homes. In one, the female videographer emitted a small yelp when the man raised his sledge. "Hold on, lemme get over here," she said, moving behind him so the camera had a clearer view of the wall, painted the yellow of cake batter. The woman cried out excitedly upon the first several blows. But the man's progress was disappointingly gradual. He struck the wall again and again. After a few minutes he stopped, chest heaving. The dust slowly settled. There was a distinct sense of anticlimax. "Good job, babe," the woman said, almost sarcastically.

Now, armed with a rudimentary understanding of demolition, Reese entered a rabbit pen and selected a twenty-pound sledge, a mattock, a pair of safety goggles, and a mask. She carried the tools to the shelter's temple. She lifted the sledge and connected it with the drywall, which yielded easily, like thick cardboard. She grabbed an edge and tore a panel down from the wall, working until she'd exposed the house's blond bones and beyond them the concrete bricks of the shelter.

Reese touched her lips to the cool surface, darting out her tongue to taste its skin. She reached her right hand down the front of her jeans, and found herself slick with arousal.

Her phone buzzed in her back pocket. *Done,* Mark had texted. She replaced the plastic-wrapped garments on the rack, returned the tools she had used, and got in the car.

Mark was in good spirits. He talked nonstop on the drive home.

"We had a breakthrough tonight with 'Heliotrope,'" he said. This was the last song of the album, a ten-minute instrumental track that Psilocybin hoped would encapsulate the complex mood and narrative thrust of the first twelve songs.

"Great," Reese said. Mark continued to describe the difficulties they'd had in mastering the song, the dozens of abortive takes over the past two weeks and the transcendent quality of tonight's recording session. Reese watched the amber sticks of the dashboard clock rearrange themselves into new minutes. She replayed in her mind the moment her sledge had contacted the drywall, piercing its membrane, causing damage that any casual observer could see.

The next evening promised to be even more productive for Psilocybin. In the morning Mark announced he'd be staying late at the studio, and Reese insisted he take the car so he would be free to stay as long as he needed to. She hoped he wouldn't come home at all. Earlier in the summer, he'd crashed a few nights in the feed store, on an air mattress set in the aisle between shelves of moldering bean sacks. Back then she'd objected to spending the night alone in the house, but now it suited her purposes.

Reese knew she would need heavier artillery for the concrete of the shelter. From her research, more videos of men brutalizing walls, she determined she would need a jackhammer, which Todd's crew was using on the foundation job. It was a long, turquoise-bodied implement that reminded Reese of the hand blender she used to make smoothies. She carried it to the shelter wall and plugged its thick red cord into an outlet. She chose a spot on the concrete a few feet from the ground and angled the snout down before flipping the switch.

The hammer bucked. Reese clung to its handles, her skin and teeth set to a fine vibration. The chisel of the hammer gnawed into the concrete. Dust shot into her face, obscuring the lenses of her goggles. Despite the mask, she began to cough. She felt resistance, and finally release as the innermost layer was breached, at which point her body shuddered with a confusing, fragmented orgasm. She turned off the hammer, breathing heavily. She poked her pinkie into the small hole she had made. She put her nose to the hole and smelled plaster and earth, the stagnant shelter air.

Reese made two more holes to form a triangle, then used the mattock to tear the stone loose. Pieces fell from above. Rubble accumulated at her feet. She did not stop until she had created a hole large enough to clamber through. She shone her flashlight inside. As the dust settled, she could make out the Shop-Vac, the crate of wine, and the box of crackers. Reese climbed through the hole. She sat on the

floor of the shelter, exhausted and satisfied. After a few minutes, she curled up on her side, resting her ear on the cool
concrete.

The Honda rumbled in the driveway. Reese crawled from the
shelter and ran upstairs, to the en suite bathroom. She got
into the shower and began loofahing concrete dust from her
skin. Mark soon found her. His form was blurred by the rain
glass of the shower door. Slowly, he began to remove his
clothes. Smears of color—the red and black of his flannel,
the indigo of his Levi's—ceded, piece by piece, to the uniform pink of his flesh.

Mark entered the shower. Reese closed her eyes and
plunged her face into falling water. Mark pressed his body
against her back and began kissing her neck. Reese cringed.

"I'm sorry I've been so busy," he said. "Once we're done
with 'Heliotrope' I'll have a lot more free time. Maybe we
can spend a weekend in Chicago."

Mark worked his hand beneath her right forearm. She allowed him to cup her breast for a moment before she turned,
kissed his cheekbone, and said she wanted to get dry.

During the third day of work on the house's foundation, a
boy from Todd's team climbed the stairs and paused on his
way to the bathroom. Reese had noticed his gaze tracking her
whenever she went down to the basement to take lunch re-
quests or replenish their pitcher of iced tea. He was thickset,
with dark eyes and a full mouth, his pudgy cheeks dusted
with freckles. Whenever he came upstairs, he stared at her

and she graced him with a stiff smile before turning back to her screen. Today he was bolder, probably reasoning that this was his last chance at meaningful contact, the kind he might brag about to his friends beneath a canopy of bong vapor. He lingered on the threshold of the living room at the line where hardwood met carpet.

The boy spoke but Reese had headphones on and didn't hear. She paused the dungeon orgy that was pumping and straining to its inevitable conclusion on her laptop screen. "How are you?" he said, the tone of his question souring in his embarrassment at having to repeat it.

"Fine. Just working."

"What do you do?" She could tell he wanted to come closer but knew he shouldn't step onto the carpet in his work boots.

"I write copy for a porn website."

"Sounds cool."

"It's not." She shut her laptop and placed it beside her on the couch. She crossed the room and stood with her back against the wall, light switches digging into her spine. "Will you come back tomorrow? I have another job I need done."

"Um, sure," he said. "Have you talked about it with Todd?"

"We don't need Todd," she said. "It's a small job. I thought you could do it all on your own."

The boy's face flushed, and she hurried to say, "It's just a wall. There's a big hole in a wall I need fixed. Can you do that?"

The boy said he thought he could handle it.

When he arrived the next day, Reese pretended not to notice the boy was wearing a button-down shirt, his face freshly shaven. She showed him the hole she had made in the wall of the shelter. The price he quoted seemed high, but she didn't bother negotiating. She told him she needed it done the following day. She wouldn't be home but would leave the front door unlocked for him.

"Okay," he said slowly, as though unwilling to accept this as the extent of her desire.

"Please clean up after yourself," she said. "Put the clothes back on the rack. Don't leave any trace."

"No problem." They were in the foyer now. He shifted from foot to foot, palpating the razor burn along his jawline. "Is that all?"

Reese deadened her eyes. "Just the wall," she said. "Let me write you a check."

Reese hid herself under the sleeping bag when she heard his boots on the stairs. She waited for light to shaft through the hole. But the boy was not curious. He got right to work. Reese lay on the cold floor of the shelter, surrounded by the groceries and supplies she had gathered. A bucket for her waste. A flashlight, extra batteries, and a dozen votive candles. A sleeping bag and pillow. A corkscrew so that later she could get drunk.

She listened to the boy pack and smooth fresh concrete into the hole. He worked for a short stretch, then went back upstairs. She imagined him standing in the kitchen, nibbling discreet edges off things from their fridge.

Soon he was back, the sounds muted now as he patched the drywall. When he was finished she heard the boy put his tools away, then cough and spit on the floor. She listened to his footsteps fade up the stairs. Only after she heard his car sputter and peel out in a spray of gravel did she stand and press her hands against the new wall. The concrete would take several days to cure, but in the meantime the drywall would protect her. The boy had done a fine job.

Night fell outside the shelter. Reese lit a candle. She ate a sleeve of rosemary crackers, drank half a bottle of red wine, and made use of the bucket. Before falling asleep, she inserted foam plugs into her ears so she wouldn't hear when, in an hour or two days or a week, someone arrived at the door of her shelter, and knocked.

The Head in the Floor

To be honest things weren't going so well even before the head started coming out of my floor. I was unemployed and universally hated thanks to some choices I'd made. Afternoons I'd go sit in this median strip a few blocks from my apartment and write things in my notebook while cars barreled past. Sometimes I brought a guitar.

First it was just a soft patch. I figured maybe, you know, the floor was rotting. What did I know about floors?

I thought of men I could text to ask them about this like, bruise in my floor. I was a little hard up in terms of people to text because, well, like I said.

First I texted this guy Lee. I texted Lee saying there's a soft spot in my floor and could he come over and check it out, does he know something about floors?

When he came over Lee was wearing a nice shirt and like, product in his hair. Maybe even cologne.

Lee pressed his fingers into the soft spot in my floor. Then he kind of like, recoiled and said I should call my landlord. I wasn't going to do that. I've lived in this apartment six years and never once have I called the landlord. One of my windows won't open and another won't close. The toilet appears to be eating itself. The lock on my door is broken sometimes. Sometimes I'm trapped in my apartment for days until the humidity drops and I can slide the deadbolt out again.

Lee asked if I wanted to like, watch a movie and I said no and he looked sad but said okay. He left and I put a towel over the soft spot in my floor.

After a few days I could no longer deny that the towel was bulging up in the middle. So I peeled it back and there was like. The top of a head. With straight brown hair. It was cresting, you know, like when they talk about the baby's head poking out. Out of the woman. It was the same thing, but you know. My floor.

I texted this guy Chris and was like. Hey Chris.

So Chris came over. He also seemed sort of a little bit more dressed up than the last time I saw him, though to be honest I don't remember when that was or who Chris even is. He brought pizza. So I'm like, that's cool. Better than Lee. Lee didn't bring anything. When he saw the top of the head he—I mean Chris—well, you could tell he wasn't expecting that. He brought his tools, too, I didn't mention that. Both pizza and tools. Way better than Lee.

I asked Chris to touch it, you know, to see if it was warm. He said he didn't want to. I said this is why I asked him to come over. This is what I needed him for. So Chris looked like he was going to throw up or like collapse in upon himself like a dead star due to this sudden revelation of like, the harrowing absurdity, futility, pain. I mean of existence. He laid the towel carefully over the head. I thought you just wanted to hang out, he said. He sounded like. Wounded. He took the pizza with him.

So at this point I was starting to regret that everyone hates me and how all I do all day is sit in the median, this like three-foot-wide strip of grass between six lanes of traffic, and pretend I'm writing in a notebook or pretend I'm playing guitar. Pretty soon I'd run out of guys to text to come over and help me with the human head coming out of my floor.

The towel helped. I'm not going to sit here and tell you the towel did nothing.

The last number in my phone of a man who did not yet know me well enough to hate me was Brandon, who I probably went on some sort of date with at some point in my life. I think Brandon said we should hang out again and I was like, yeah, and then when he named an actual day of the week I never responded and deleted all our texts.

Brandon didn't bring anything and he seemed annoyed. I wasn't sure why he came but I was glad to have him there when I lifted the towel.

You could just make out the upper edge of the eyebrows. Brandon agreed it was a man's head. You could tell. It's not just because of the size. I'm saying. You can tell.

I asked Brandon if he'd touch the top of the head to see if it was warm. Meaning, alive. Brandon said no. I said, someone has to. He said, it's your floor. I gave him this look. He sighed and told me how when we went on a date four years ago I was really rude. I tried to remember this date. I remembered lots of other dates, but none of those guys' faces looked like Brandon's, not really. I felt like I could grab Brandon's wrist and put his hand on the head before he realized what was happening. Then we'd know.

I told Brandon I was sorry, even though I couldn't remember this date we supposedly went on. Well, I said. Would you want to stay here with me while the head rises out of my floor? Of course I expected him to say no. Any normal person would abandon me to this horror that is after all my burden and no one else's. Or tell me to call the landlord. Which, you know. That's off the table.

But Brandon got this look like of utter defeat and sighed again and went. Yeah. Okay.

So I broke my median routine and now I stay in the apartment with Brandon all day. We mostly ignore each other. He works on his laptop because he's a freelancer. I don't know what kind. He told me but I guess I didn't care. Sometimes I look over at him and wonder what fundamental and overpowering sadness there is inside of him that compels him to stay here with me while the head rises from my floor. But I'm not going to say anything, because like. What if he leaves.

It's been five days since Brandon joined me. The head continues to rise. We lift the towel every two hours to check on it. It's rising at the rate of around a quarter inch per day. So by 6:00 A.M. tomorrow. There'll be the eyes.

This is like, what it's all been building up to. We're excited but we also feel like maybe. You know, maybe it's too late now. Maybe before, someone could have done something. Something could have been done.

The eyes are blue and like, alert. They're blinking at what you might call normal intervals. I mean to say they're alive.

Looking at us. They seem like they're in an okay mood. Like, not tortured, at least. That's a relief. That answers at least one of our questions.

Now that we have the eyes we feel like we can talk to the head like we're all in this thing together. Hey buddy, we say. How's it going? We only ask to be polite. The head can't respond because its mouth is still in the floor. If it even has a mouth. Sometimes we tell the head stories about our lives. When the head gets bored of our stories its eyes close and we stop. We don't put the towel back over the head. It seems like now there's the matter of like. Human rights. We figure it'll be a few more days and there'll be the mouth. And then we'll clear some things up.

All along I've been hoping it'll be like six months and then the whole man is up out of the floor. I imagine he's wearing a suit and he'll straighten his tie and shake my hand and walk out my door and the floor will kind of neatly seal up after him. So like I won't have to tell my landlord after all or adjust in any small way the constituents of this miserable life that is after all my burden and no one else's.

But days pass and it's still just the eyes, and they're always awake and staring at me and Brandon, unless we're standing behind the head. It isn't rising anymore. The head. Like, it's stuck. Or maybe that's all there is. Maybe it's been just the top third of a head all along.

After a few weeks we put the towel back over the head. Since then it's been a few more months. Brandon seems to live with me. I've started going out to the median strip again. I don't know. We don't really talk. Me and Brandon. We've never touched each other. At first I thought he wanted to. But now I'm not really too sure.

Tahoe

We'd been warned not to ride the ATVs straight up the hill, but we did, and one of us, I think it was Joel, toppled backwards and his ATV fell on top of him. The night before, we'd gone into the creek behind the cabin and come out with leeches on our calves. We pried them off with spoon handles and tossed them on the coals of the grill. They were still alive and their bodies sizzled and popped as they burned and I wondered if anyone else felt bad about that.

We were in Tahoe for a bachelor party. I'm not sure which one of us was getting married, that trip. I want to say it was Jim. But Jim got married after me, and I remember that weekend trying to call my girlfriend at the time, Bonnie, who went a little nuts if I was out of touch too long. It was after the leeches had shriveled to husks on the coals and I was roaming the woods climbing foothills trying to get a bar or two of service just to shoot off a text to Bonnie so she wouldn't get drunk and start calling ex-boyfriends. I didn't marry Bonnie, of course. I married a woman who needs me less, and all in all it's worked out.

They say at the deepest part of Lake Tahoe the water goes down over sixteen hundred feet. They say the cold of the lake at such depths can preserve a human body in perfect condition for centuries. One of us, maybe Mike, or it could have been Jim, or Joel, or even me for that matter, said we should rent some scuba gear and see what we could find. But only Mike and Jim, or maybe Mike and Joel, but definitely Mike, were certified for scuba and the next day we ended up getting the ATVs instead and one of us toppled his ATV onto himself, falling backwards going up a hill. Come to think of it, it might have been me the ATV fell on. I remember hard blue sky through a fringe of trees and gasoline ribboning the air and the pressure of a tire on my chest.

So I know the trip happened before I was married, while I was still dating Bonnie, and that there were four of us: Jim, Joel, Mike, and me. Then again I remember our friend Emile, who lives in Sacramento, popping into the cabin the first night with a bottle of Johnnie Walker Black, so maybe it was the trip we took later, to San Luis Obispo, because we didn't meet Emile until 2008, and I think Jim got married in '06. We might have rented ATVs in SLO and taken them on the beach, but it wouldn't make sense for Emile to come all the way to SLO from Sac, seeing as he wasn't that good of friends with any of us. So it must have been the last trip, when Mike got married in 2010, and Emile popped in, but Mike definitely got married after me, so then how to explain my searching for service in the forest so I could text Bonnie? At any rate I definitely remember forest and not beach while we drew close to whichever one of us was screaming under the ATV, whether it was me, Joel, Jim, Mike, or maybe even Emile.

After the ATV accident we went back to the cabin and made dinner. We each assigned ourselves a little job. I prepped the skewers. Jim was on the grill. It was Mike's family's cabin, or maybe Jim's. Probably not Joel's because I think Joel's parents live in Boston. It's possible it was my family's cabin, because we do have one in Tahoe. Anyway we went down to the basement after eating and threw darts and got drunk on Corona and whiskey and blasted Zeppelin and pissed in a storm drain out the sliding door by the patio furniture instead of walking upstairs to the bathroom.

Around ten a stranger knocked on the door and asked us to turn down the music. We invited him in for a beer. He was maybe fifty, tall and broad-shouldered, the type of dude who might have played football in college. He carried a wooden walking stick carved like a snake with a bowl built into the head. We sat in the living room and smoked the stranger's weed while he drank our beer. We took turns putting our lips on the little snake mouth. We asked the man if the rumors were true about the Mafia dumping bodies in the lake in the fifties and the man said he didn't really know because he'd lied to us about living down the road. We asked where did he live and he said Reno. He asked did we mind if he stayed the night? We said sorry but he couldn't stay, this was a private event, our friend Mike or Jim or Joel was getting married.

Around 3:00 A.M. we told the guy straight up that he

needed to leave but he wouldn't move from the couch and we were worried about him stealing the Blu-ray so one of us brought out a rifle and pointed it at him and told him to get out. And the stranger took a hunting knife out of his waistband and lunged at the guy with the gun and the guy with the gun, maybe Mike or Jim, or maybe even me—but probably not Joel if he was the one injured in the ATV accident, seeing how his arm was in a sling and he wouldn't be able to hold the rifle—whoever had the gun pulled the trigger and killed the stranger and we rowed the stranger's body out on the lake as far as we could by the light of a full moon and dropped it in the part we hoped was deepest, maybe not sixteen hundred feet but plenty deep, deep enough. In the morning I was in charge of making the omelets and Mike made the pancakes and Jim made the coffee and Joel just sat there groaning from the pain of his arm that had been injured in the ATV accident. Or maybe I made pancakes and Mike made omelets. Jim definitely made the coffee, though.

I just tried to find Joel's number in my phone and set some of this straight and my wife asked what I was doing and I told her and she said, what are you talking about, Joel died in that ATV accident at Jim's bachelor party in '08, and anyway, my wife said, it's too late at night to be making phone calls.

The Bone Ward

B y night our bones dissolve into our blood like sugar in tea. We sleep in anti-gravity pods with slick outer shells and vinyl interiors, our limbs held by Velcro straps, our torsos bound by cuirasses that force our lungs to expand. Classical music pipes through speakers, masking the ventilators' hum. Outside, coyotes range over the Montana plains, scratching and whining, searching for dead things to eat. As the sun rises, our skeletons stitch themselves back together.

Since my arrival four months ago, I've been the only woman on the Bone Ward. With me are Frankie, a tattooed Porsche mechanic from Oakland; Rick, a bald, portly man who owns a chain of grocery stores in central Florida; Tim, a wheaten-haired twenty-year-old who grew up on an Idaho farm; and Bradley, the one I love, and who I hope will love me, in time. Bradley is a musician, tall with jewel-green eyes, long fingers, and wavy hair grown just past his ears. He is my conception of the perfect man, as if manifested through years of consolatory fantasies. Whenever our eyes meet across the dining table or the TV room, my heart wrings itself out, flushing my extremities with blood heat.

The Bone Ward belongs to a loose collective of quarantines for esoteric diseases. Before I came, Bradley was seeing a woman in the Epidermal Ward, half a mile across the arid, crumbly land pocked with juniper and saltbush. Her skin was zebra-striped, the dark bands tender as deep bruises. When they tried to have sex, Bradley grazed a dark stripe and she screamed, alerting the orderlies to his presence.

"I like that I can touch you wherever I want," Bradley said, the first time we had sex. I lay on crinkling butcher paper in an exam room. He ran his hands over my body, thumbs pressing hard into my flesh.

The cause of Total Nocturnal Bone Loss remains a mystery. On the day I arrived, the men questioned me, trying to find a common thread in our stories that might explain why we'd developed TNBL. We could find no obvious link. Frankie joked that my arrival was a promising sign, that more "chicks" were surely on their way to the ward. There is no cure yet, but Dr. Will's treatment regimen has enabled the afflicted to lead relatively normal lives. Two patients have been discharged from the Bone Ward so far; I'll likely be the third. My bones now stay nearly solid through the night, and Dr. Will believes I'll be ready to go home in another month or two. But I'm in no hurry to go back to my life in New York. I dread returning to my copywriting job at a slick midtown ad agency, where I used my English literature degree to hawk creams, gels, and cosmetic procedures to insecure women. I dread resuming my rituals of maintenance and control—the keto dieting and master cleanses, the Bikram yoga and Soul-Cycle, the monthly clockwork of organic facials and gel manicures and Brazilian waxes.

I dread, most of all, the happy hours and dinner parties with my girlfriends, nights of fatalistic bonding over the dearth of good single men as we push deeper into our thirties. My secret hope is to leave the ward with Bradley, but he is at least a few months behind me, in the scheme of recovery. So I've been stalling, treating my body carelessly and skipping the occasional dose of bone-girding meds, so that I won't be forced to leave before properly securing Bradley's love.

Today is my 124th day on the ward. I lie in my pod, inhaling the last wisps of morphine fog, and push the call button so our nurse, Lily, knows I'm awake. A new patient is scheduled to arrive today—a woman, Lily told us. I look forward to no longer being the sole object of the men's desire for sex and nurturance and everything else women are to men. It will be a relief, to have another woman to share the burden of jokes and innuendos. But a childish part of me feels possessive, as if these men belong to me. Part of me hopes the new woman will be unviable in some way—old or deformed or happily married.

"Morning," Lily says, lifting the top hatch of my pod. Lily is the sole nurse on the ward. She lives near Billings and drives in each morning before dawn, to be on hand when we wake in our pods. Though she's only in her midforties, she's become like a mother to all of us. She runs her hands under my body, peeling my sticky flesh from the upholstery. My thin pajamas are soaked through with the fluids of reconstitution that seeped from my pores during the night. Lily takes my elbow and helps me out of the pod. We go to an exam room, where she massages the skin over my bones, smoothing my skeleton into alignment. She measures my pelvis and reports that it's crooked by a few centimeters.

"You need to take it easy," she says, and I know she's referring to my trysts with Bradley. Last night we had sex in this exam room. My gaze drifts over the locked drawers of needles and gauze and I remember how I held the handles, my body folded at the waist, Bradley's fingers gripping my hipbones.

Lily's concern is justified. Our bones grow increasingly pliable as night deepens, and strenuous activity near bedtime can throw our skeletons out of whack. In a worst-case scenario, my body could be damaged enough to necessitate a stint in the Iron Skeleton. I promise Lily I'll be more careful. She nods sternly, and discharges me to the women's shower room, where I wash and put on a fresh set of scrubs. I go to the kitchen, make coffee, and pour it into white mugs on which we've written our names in Sharpie. I know how each man likes his coffee, and I have the mugs ready for them on the table as they straggle in, one by one. Bradley's hair is tousled, his eyes puffy. When he sees me, he smiles and comes over to kiss my cheek before he takes his seat at the table.

For breakfast, we eat bran flakes in whole milk, fortified orange juice, and planks of walnut bread slathered with nutritive paste. The men are silent, navigating waves of nausea and pain as their tendons and ligaments wrap and firm around new bone. I take small bites of walnut bread, averting my gaze from their downturned faces. Later, I know,

they'll be in high spirits, making crass jokes about getting
boned and deboned. It never seems to get old. Frankie has
invented bone-related nicknames for everyone: Tenderman,
Chicken Nugget, Marshmallow Dick. When I arrived, he
christened me Gumdrop, which stuck while the others' nicknames haven't; at this point, I wonder whether the men even
remember my real name.

Bradley places his hand on my thigh. We leave our cereal
unfinished and head to a disused exam room at the far end of
the corridor. We flatten the exam chair to horizontal. It's narrow, and we have to squeeze to fit, Bradley tucked behind me,
molding his body to mine. Earlier in my time here, such feats
of balance and core strength would have been impossible for
me this early in the morning. But now I am almost back to
normal. Bradley runs his hands under the starched cotton of
my V-neck top, massaging my breasts. He undoes the draw-
string at my waist, and makes a hum of contentment when
he finds I'm already wet. I turn to face him, my lips grazing
his neck. I grip him until he comes.

I rinse my hand in the sink, catching a slice of my face in
the metal towel dispenser. My eyes and skin are bright, my
body vivid. I look five years younger than I did when I came
to the Bone Ward.

"Thanks," Bradley says, with ironic casualness.

"No problem."

"I'll get you back tonight. Don't feel up to it at the moment."

"Sure thing," I say. I sit beside him on the chair and rest
my head on his shoulder, our feet dangling above the floor in
matching canvas slippers.

We emerge into the corridor. The ward is horseshoe-shaped. At the end of its arms sit the two Iron Skeletons: sleek black tubes seven feet long, the sides riddled with buttons and gauges, and fitted with a panel that slides back to reveal the face of the patient inside. Most days, though, the Skeletons stand empty. They are a last resort, used in the most acute phases of the disease, or in the rare instance when our bones emerge from the night wrongly baked. Inside, highly pressurized air pumps the skeleton back into alignment, over the course of hours or days. It is a brutal process. I've never had to go there, but Bradley says it's torture.

The ward attendant, Greg, passes us, pushing a yellow janitor's bucket.

"Hi, Greg!" Bradley says, with mocking cheer. Greg scowls and keeps moving. Lily is the only real nurse here. Greg does maintenance on the ward. He cleans and restocks and hoists our bodies into the pods on nights we wait too long to strap in. I would have thought he'd get used to our condition, but he seems newly disgusted every time he sees us.

Bradley and I head to the TV room, where the bulk of our day will be spent, waiting for Dr. Will to call us in one at a time to draw our blood, take X-rays, and measure our bone density. As usual, we watch *Maury* at three. Today is a paternity test episode. A young blond woman named Amy is back for a second round, having brought another contemptuous man who insists he's not the father of her baby. A looped video of the infant appears on a screen behind them. It crawls around a studio crib, its pudgy fingers grasping for off-camera toys. The audience coos on the first few loops, but the baby's evocative power soon fades and the crowd trains its fervor on the man, JC, who sports a goatee and an oversized Billabong T-shirt.

Bradley and I sit on the loveseat, my legs slung over his lap. I straighten and grab his hand when it's time for Maury to reveal the results of the paternity test, as though it's the final, climactic moment of a sporting event.

"I bet he's the dad," Tim says—sweet, young Tim, who was struck down by TNBL just before he was heading to Indiana on a basketball scholarship. "The baby looks like him."

"The baby looks the same as all babies," Frankie says grumpily. He leans back in his chair, muscular arms crossed over his chest. Frankie's arms are covered in tattoos, an intricate patchwork of diamonds, flames, a dagger, a bird's outstretched wing. I've always wondered what his arms look like at night, the images distorted by the stretched canvas of his boneless flesh.

"What are you talking about?" Tim insists. "There's totally a resemblance."

Rick shushes them; he's sitting forward in his chair, elbows on knees, his broad back humped in a manner that would surely earn Lily's disapproval. Bradley and I exchange a smile, amused by how engaged the men are in Amy's saga. Though of course we are, too.

"JC," Maury says, pausing for suspense, "you are *not* the father."

JC leaps from his chair, whooping and unleashing a string of joyful bleeped expletives at Amy, Maury, and the studio audience. In the TV room, the men chuckle, presumably at Amy's impressive promiscuity. I laugh, too, at the ridiculous scene of JC taunting the crowd, though in my previous life I'd found the show gross.

Beneath the riotous sounds of the studio audience, we

hear the front doors of the ward open. Tim mutes the TV and we hear Lily giving the new patient a tour of the ward. The air in the room stills as we strain to listen. I'm reminded of the first day of college classes, how we waited in anticipation for our new professor to walk through the door. A female voice responds with murmurs of understanding and assent to Lily's descriptions of how the ward operates, the measures we must take to increase our chances of survival. Bradley's hand is warm in mine. I give it a squeeze.

Lily and the new patient enter the TV room, and I feel my skin blanch. She's cut from the cloth of my nightmares: petite, with wide hazel eyes, caramel-colored hair, bangs cut low across her forehead. Her arms and legs are delicate, milky stems protruding from the silken edges of a blue polka-dotted dress. She wears no makeup, no jewelry, no polish on her nails. My career writing ad copy to exploit women's physical insecurities has rendered me expert in the minutiae of female beauty. In this sense, I am like a judge of pedigree dogs or horses. When I say that this woman is flawless, I do not mean it lightly. She possesses no attribute that I would, in good faith, suggest augmenting or reducing, highlighting or minimizing, smoothing or shaping or lengthening or rejuvenating or otherwise subjecting to any of the verbs I employed daily to describe the infinite ways in which a woman might fail to achieve her corporeal potential. I would not know how to sell her a thing.

The new woman stands in front of us and waves. "Hi. I'm Olivia," she chirps.

The air of the ward ripples. I turn to look at the men next to me. They are staring at Olivia with a predatory hunger that turns my stomach; how obvious and crude it looks, when directed at someone else. They each stand and introduce themselves with a gallantness that I find comical, given their usual behavior. Bradley removes his hand from mine and wipes his palm on the loveseat's upholstery before shaking Olivia's hand. He then offers her his seat.

"Hi," she says, settling in next to me and extending her hand.

Her palm is cool and dry. Even up close, the skin of her face appears poreless. When she crosses her legs, I smell baby powder and cheap drugstore sunscreen.

I watch the men observe Olivia with furtive curiosity. They pose gentle questions. With every answer, she reveals herself to be even more threatening than I had feared. Olivia comes from a small town in Tennessee. Since graduating college, she's worked as an outreach coordinator for a domestic violence shelter. She is twenty-six, the daughter of a preacher and a seamstress. She grew up singing gospel music in the Baptist church, and spent the previous summer touring the South with her cousin's bluegrass band.

"Sing us something, sweetheart," Frankie says, his voice soft for once.

"Oh, no, I'm too shy," Olivia says.

"Come on," Tim whines.

"Please," Bradley adds.

Olivia clears her throat and begins singing "Amazing Grace." My eyes tear with embarrassment for her—how cliché. But the men are rapt. Her voice is surprisingly rich and powerful, incongruous with her tiny frame. When she finishes, they applaud.

"We'll call her Starling," Frankie says.

"Our little songbird," Rick agrees.

———

It's clear that Olivia is sicker than any of us were when we came to the ward. Her slim fingers are arthritic, their joints bulbous. She walks with a careful limp. At dinner, her face is tense. She doesn't speak. I feel terrible for her; she must be in extraordinary pain.

"You should eat something, Starling," Frankie says.

Olivia shakes her head. "It's okay," she says. "I'm not feeling well."

"The food is calibrated to our bodies' needs," Bradley says, like a Boy Scout reciting survival tips. "It'll do you good."

Tim spreads marrow on Olivia's bread and offers it to her. Olivia looks like she'll cry. She raises the bread to her mouth and takes a tiny bite. Her face pales. She gags, a milky spittle pushing past her lips. She tries to gather it all in a napkin.

Bradley calls for help. Lily runs over; Greg brings the wheelchair. They lower Olivia's rubbery body into the chair. I am astonished. Her bone loss has started already, and it's not even 6:00 P.M. We watch her skeleton melt with alarming speed. Greg touches her upper arm and his glove comes away sticky with calcium sap, a by-product of bone dissolution. Her face sags into a leering putty mask. Her head droops on the wilting stem of her spine. I avert my eyes, feeling nauseous.

Olivia is wheeled off to the Iron Skeleton. We sit in an abashed silence, as if we've accidentally witnessed something private.

"Jeez," Tim says. "That was nuts."

"Poor girl," Rick says, shaking his head.

"I wouldn't wish the Iron Skeleton on my worst enemy," Bradley says.

After dinner, Bradley and I huddle on the bench in the courtyard, surrounded by spindly trees and the planters of wildflowers that we take turns plucking weeds from. Before succumbing to TNBL, Bradley was principal cellist in the Chicago Symphony. Today, he received another get-well card from members of his section. Bradley hasn't seen any of them since last summer's concert, from which he was removed on a stretcher. The cellos were playing their solo in the Largo movement of Dvořák's New World Symphony when the fingers of Bradley's left hand crumpled, his bow belching a granular, open-stringed C before clattering to the floor. The concert was halted. The audience watched, horrified, as Bradley's body melted, arms splaying, head rolling back, mouth gaping up at the stage lights.

"They never tell me anything real," Bradley says. "It's always like, 'We're thinking of you and can't wait to have you back.' That's bullshit. I'm sure they're well into auditioning for a new principal by now."

"I'm sorry," I say. "But if they do end up replacing you, you'll find something else. Any orchestra would be lucky to have you."

"Yeah, but a principal position in a major symphony isn't something you land every day," Bradley says, unwilling to be comforted.

It was Bradley who proposed the ward play music while our bones dissolve. He arranged a soothing mix of Bach, Debussy, Chopin. Over the past three months, Bradley has taught me to love classical music. At night we listen to

Stravinsky and Tchaikovsky and Beethoven on a battered CD player. A few times, I've tried reading to him from the two books of poetry I brought with me, Neruda and Dickinson, but as soon as I began a poem, Bradley's eyes would glaze, and I knew I was boring him.

"Olivia seems nice," I say, to change the subject.

"Yeah," Bradley says. "Poor thing."

"I remember how disoriented I was when I first got here," I say. I'd been sent to the ward suddenly, after dismissing my worsening symptoms for months, attributing them variously to hangovers, seasonal flus, a proliferation of candida in my gut. Some days I walked with a limp; others, I had to tease my hair to conceal a dent in my skull. Finally, on a Saturday night in December, I brought a man home from a bar in Murray Hill. He worked in finance, a cherubic, pale-eyed blond. In the morning I woke in a pool of fluid that I mistook for urine. I now know it was the excretion of bone loss. The banker was sitting at the end of the bed, staring at me. He asked what was wrong with my face. I had slept on my stomach, my face pressed into the mattress. I raised my fingers to find my nose flattened against my cheeks. My left shoulder had been wrenched from its socket, arm dangling outward. My left hand was gnarled from where it had been crushed under the weight of my hip during reconstitution. The fingers jutted at wild angles, like the arms of a Joshua tree. In the emergency room, a bewildered young doctor called the CDC, and by evening I was on a flight to Billings, bound for the Bone Ward.

I've withheld this story from Bradley, worrying he'll be turned off by the part about me fucking a man I'd met at a bar the same night. I want to tell him now, though; he's made

himself vulnerable, telling me about his fears of being replaced, and I have the urge to reciprocate.

But Bradley preempts me. "I can't wait to get out of this
fucking place," he says. "Dr. Will says it should only be a few
more months."

"That's great," I say, forcing the words around the ache in
my throat. I feel betrayed whenever Bradley talks about leaving. "What do you think you'll do next?"

Bradley stares across the courtyard. I can tell he's choosing
his words carefully.

"Who knows what'll happen," he says. "Maybe I'll get a
job in New York."

It is the closest he's gotten to suggesting a life together
outside of the ward. "That would be great," I say, aiming for
a breezy tone.

Bradley chucks me on the arm. "Come on, Gumdrop," he
says. "I owe you an orgasm."

We bring the CD player into an exam room and Bradley
puts on Rachmaninoff's Piano Concerto no. 2. Amid the
moody interplay of piano and strings, Bradley uses his mouth
and fingers to make me come. I then help him climb into his
pod. I position the ventilator over his face, strap on his cuirass, and watch as the tubes raise the wall of his chest. His
green eyes gaze up at me in the moment before I lower the
lid, sealing him in for the night.

I climb into my own pod, though it will be hours before
my bones soften. Dr. Will told me I don't need to use the ventilator anymore. I sometimes miss the sensation of total bone
loss, its own kind of orgasm. A forced surrender, a sudden
lack—like a floor dropping out, air and light rushing into a
room.

———

For three days, Olivia is confined to the Skeleton. On the third afternoon, we're sitting in the TV room watching *Judge Joe Brown* when a wheelchair squeaks behind us. Greg wheels Olivia over and parks her next to me.

"Thank you, Greg," Olivia says. Greg grins awkwardly and slinks away.

Olivia turns to me. "How are you feeling today?" she asks.

"I'm fine," I say, both charmed and irritated by her kindness.

"How are *you* feeling?" Tim asks Olivia.

"Oh, I've been worse," Olivia said. "You all know how it is."

Once again, Olivia's presence seems to have displaced the air in the room. I catch Bradley sneaking looks at her. He keeps a few inches of distance between us on the couch.

Lily walks back into the TV room. "I forgot to tell you, dear," she says, to Olivia. "You've received some packages."

"My guitar?" Olivia says, perking up.

"Among other things. You're a popular lady."

My skin prickles with envy. In my time here, I've received only one item, a postcard from my friend Emily, sent from Sicily, where she and her new husband were honeymooning. Emily insisted on having my new address, when I told her I would be unable to attend her wedding due to a sudden medical issue. I was vague with people back home regarding my departure. A few emails from coworkers, received within my first weeks on the ward, suggested they thought I'd been sent to drug rehab. I told my mother I was suffering from an acute form of osteoporosis—not true, but an analogue I knew she would accept and not panic over. I text her once a week, to let her know I'm alive, but she doesn't seem worried. She's busy with my stepdad and their teenage son, who's already been kicked out of the two best private high schools in their Connecticut town.

Olivia shrugs, self-effacingly. "They're probably all from people in my dad's congregation," she says. "I've asked him a million times to keep me out of his sermons, but he can't help himself. Especially now, I'm sure."

Lily nods. "Well, they're stacked in the entryway, whenever you want to take a look."

"Should we go get them, Starling?" Frankie says, after Lily leaves.

"Not right now, I don't think," Olivia says. "I'm pretty exhausted."

"You play guitar?" Bradley asks.

"I did," Olivia says. "I don't think I'll be able to anymore, though. Not for a while."

"Will you teach me?" Bradley asks. His tone is playful, but I know he's serious.

"Sure," Olivia says, beaming. "I'd love to."

It's my night to cook dinner. I prepare a meal from Dr. Will's binder of recipes. I scramble eggs, grind the shells with a pestle, and sprinkle the powder into sautéed spinach. I assemble a spread of white cheddar, flaxseed crackers, marrow, and sardines in olive oil. I fill our mugs with warm bone broth, selecting an unmarked mug from the cabinet for Olivia. I consider writing her name on it, but decide not to. I know she would lavish me with gratitude for such a gesture, and the prospect embarrasses me. If she wants to claim a mug, she can ask.

I ferry the food from kitchen to table. The men coo in a parody of appreciation, and for a moment I'm reassured that nothing has changed.

"Your hair looks nice that way, Gumdrop," Tim says. Before cooking, I had pulled my hair into a bun.

"Like a ballerina," Rick adds.

"Very pretty," Olivia agrees, and I blush; her praise carries more weight than the men's, her tone so earnest.

We eat.

"The spinach is good tonight, Gumdrop," Frankie says. "Lots of lemon. Just how I like it."

"She's a good cook," Bradley says, and I blush again.

"She'd be prettier if she smiled, though," Frankie teases, as he does every night. In response I roll my eyes and make a point of frowning.

"What about you, Starling?" Rick says, his face softening as he looks at Olivia. "Will you give us a smile?"

It's a joke, because Olivia is already grinning. "You're all too much," she says with a laugh. "Leave us poor girls alone."

She trains her smile at me, and I force myself to smile back. I want to like Olivia. I'm aware of the ugliness of women who are not interested in friendships with other women; women who claim they only get along with men. Yet when I look at Olivia, my blood seethes. I hate her for how she could ruin my life, without malice, simply by being herself. She could take Bradley from me. She wouldn't even have to try.

The night is warm, and Tim proposes shooting hoops in the courtyard before dark. It's Bradley's night to do dishes, but I see that he wants to go. I tell him I'll take his shift.

"Are you sure?" Bradley says.

"Yep," I say.

"I'll pick up your Thursday shift," he says, and I nod, already knowing that he'll forget, and that I won't remind him.

When the others leave, Olivia and Rick remain seated. They seem to have fallen into an intense conversation, and I give them privacy. As I ferry plates to the kitchen, I hear Rick tell Olivia about his wife, who left him after the onset of TNBL. Rick's wife was repulsed by his illness, the acrid smell released by the dissolution of bone, the fluid pooled under him when he woke. She believed these were symptoms of a sexually transmitted disease, which gave her a pretext to leave him.

I've avoided Rick as if his gloom were a contagion, but Olivia sits with him long after dinner, asking questions, encouraging him to confide in her. I stand near the door, keeping the water at a low pitch so I can hear Olivia's softly reassuring voice.

"That's so unfair," she tells Rick. "I'm sorry you've had to go through all that." I feel guilty now, for never taking the time to listen to Rick. I have been wholly focused on Bradley, and I wonder if the other men have resented me for it.

I clear Rick's and Olivia's plates from the table last, not wanting to interrupt.

"Thank you," Olivia says, when I take her plate. Her face tilts up at me like a sunflower. I curve my lips in a toothless smile. I scrub pots until the joints of my fingers burn.

The next day, Olivia is well enough to sit with us in the TV room. *Maury* is showing another paternity episode: Amy's back for a third round. The man she's brought today is younger than the others. He's skinny, with buzzed hair and crusts of healing acne in the hollows of his cheeks. His face rests in a sneer.

Olivia and I sit on the loveseat, the men perched on folding chairs in a semicircle around us. "Tyler," Maury intones, "you are *not* the father." Tyler jumps up from his chair and does a touchdown dance on the stage. The crowd erupts. In the TV room, the men snicker, as usual. Tim and Frankie high-five, as if a part of this hateful victory belongs to them.

"This show is disgusting," Olivia says softly. She leaves the room. The men fall silent, chastened. I've thought the same thing many times about *Maury*, but kept this opinion to myself, because I enjoyed our collective indulgence in trashy TV shows. We continue watching, but the mood has soured. At the next commercial break, Bradley gets up and leaves without a word. I assume he's gone to the bathroom, but when he doesn't come back after twenty minutes, I go looking. Through the hall window, I see him sitting with Olivia on the bench in the courtyard. I stand by the window, listening to her sing a jazzy version of "Swing Low, Sweet Chariot." Bradley keeps the beat with finger snaps.

The next afternoon, Bradley forgoes TV again in order to sit with Olivia in the courtyard. During quiet parts of the shows, we can hear him picking out melodies on Olivia's guitar. Every note nips at my skin. I turn up the volume on the TV until Rick complains.

This pattern persists all week. Bradley and I continue having sex most mornings. He still greets me affectionately, and sits next to me during meals. But he spends more and more of his free time with Olivia. Sometimes when I pass by the window, I see Bradley holding the guitar awkwardly while Olivia coaxes his cello-calloused fingers into the proper configurations. Other times, she's singing while Bradley jots notes in his Moleskine. But often, they are simply sitting and talking, as Bradley and I used to.

One night at dinner, Bradley and Olivia announce that they've begun collaborating on a music project. They're both excited, aglow with creative adrenaline; my chest aches with jealousy, though I pretend to be happy for them.

I stop Bradley as he exits the dining room.

"We never spend time together anymore," I say, wincing at how I sound—like a nagging, needy girlfriend.

Bradley sighs, as if he's known he would have to submit to this conversation at some point. He explains that it's the first time in months that he's felt artistically fulfilled; that it's the most fundamental part of his identity, and only now does he realize how depressed he's been without making music.

"I'm glad you're feeling inspired," I say. I can't quite rid my voice of hurt, but he doesn't seem to register it.

"Thanks," he says, beaming at me. "I think you're really going to dig what we're working on. It's a lot more innovative than I'm used to. Obviously." He laughs.

"Edgier than Mozart," I say.

"Something like that."

I am trying not to cry. Bradley finally notices I'm upset. "Aw, come on, Gumdrop," he says, drawing me in for a hug. "We've gotta work again tonight, but I'll swing by later and see what you're up to."

Bradley joins me and Tim in the TV room around 9:00 P.M.,

presumably after strapping Olivia into her pod. We're watching an old John Cusack movie from the ward's DVD collection. Bradley sits beside me on the couch. He slings his arm around my shoulder, but his posture is stiff, his leg tapping with restless energy. I have rarely felt a person's absence so acutely.

Another week passes. At breakfast one morning, I realize Bradley and I haven't had sex in five days. Later, while he's washing dishes, I take his hand and pull him into the bathroom attached to the kitchen. We have sex quickly, impersonally, while standing. After he comes, Bradley will barely look at me. He wipes his cock on a paper towel, then pulls up his scrubs and goes to the sink to wash his hands, erasing all trace of me.

"What's wrong?" I say.

"Nothing," Bradley says, turning suddenly, as if he'd forgotten I'm here. "What do you mean?"

"You're in love with her, aren't you?" I say impulsively.

Bradley gives me a look he's never given me before—a side-glance of contempt I remember from previous boyfriends, which would inevitably mark the start of a long unraveling.

"We've been over this," Bradley says. "Nothing has changed. I've just been focused on this project. I'm really excited about it. I hoped you'd be happy for me."

"I am," I say. "Of course. But what about me, Bradley?"

He pauses. "I don't think I'm in a position right now to be responsible for anyone else's needs," he says coolly. "This isn't exactly an environment that's conducive to a serious relationship. I assumed that was obvious."

"Who said anything about a serious relationship?" I say, floundering.

"Well, that's what it sounds like," Bradley says. He pulls another towel from the dispenser and begins drying his hands. "Listen, Gumdrop. You know I enjoy spending time with you. But I just can't deal with this kind of pressure right now."

"I'm sorry," I say, cringing at how desperate I sound. "I didn't mean to pressure you."

But it's too late. Bradley throws the wadded towel in the trash and moves to the door. "I think maybe it's best if we cool it for a little while," he says. "At least until the album is done."

After Bradley and I separate, the other men seem to withdraw from me as well. Frankie no longer bothers asking me to smile. At dinner each night, he instead says, "Hey, Starling, you're prettier when you smile," and Olivia flashes him a huge grin. Her joke is an inversion of mine, complying where I had refused. One night, I snap. When Frankie says his dumb line and Olivia smiles, on cue, like a well-trained dog, I say, "She's pretty whether she smiles or not."

I feel the men bristle against me. Olivia giggles and places her dry hand on mine.

"It's okay, hon," she says. "Frankie doesn't mean it that way."

We finish our food in silence. Later that night, I stand in

the darkened hall, watching Bradley as he sits next to Olivia's pod. He reads to her from a book of Whitman poems she brought in her floral-print duffel. I reflect, bitterly, that even Olivia's taste in poetry is more appealing than mine. He's placed the CD player at his feet, and I can just make out the Rachmaninoff suite unspooling beneath his ridiculous poetry-voice.

Tim and I watch a horror movie in the TV room—one in which a meagerly clothed woman runs through a forest, chased by a murderer, her cleavage smeared with blood. I watch the scenes of gore with dull eyes, the screen of my mind retaining the image of Bradley at Olivia's pod. I had considered Rachmaninoff significant to our relationship—it was Bradley's go-to accompaniment for sex—but he has re-purposed "our song" like it meant nothing. A few weeks ago, this would have wounded me, but I feel eerily calm. The thing I most feared has already happened, and I am now able to spectate on the particulars of my own rejection from a slight remove. I almost convince myself that it's a relief, to no longer have something to lose.

Tim's bones begin to soften and he's forced to return to his pod before the movie ends. I wait for the credits to roll, then stand and stretch. It's 11:00 P.M. and my bones are still firm. I could leave the ward tomorrow, go back to New York. But that would mean giving up on Bradley completely. Though my rational mind tells me it's hopeless, my heart clings to contradictory evidence—his insistence that there is nothing romantic between him and Olivia, and his promise to reeval-uate our relationship once the album is finished. There is hope for us, my heart insists, as long as I remain on the ward.

Aside from the hum of machinery that enables us to survive the night, the ward is silent; Greg is probably outside smoking, or asleep on his cot in the break room. I must pass Olivia's pod on the way to my own. The instant the idea occurs to me, my body reacts. Suddenly I'm moving to the back of Olivia's pod and pulling the plug that powers the anti-gravity in one quick motion, like tearing a root from the earth. Immediately, I regret it; there is not even a moment of satisfaction, only horror at the damage I might have caused. The anti-gravity keeps everything in place; without it, the pressure on her organs could kill her immediately. I bend down and grab at the cord, but it's fallen into a gap between the pod and the wall. At least ten seconds pass before I can get the plug back in. I feel the whoosh of the anti-gravity powering up. Above me, Debussy ends and Bach begins.

I consider confessing, finding Greg and urging him to call Dr. Will. I could say I tripped over the cord. I could say I fell asleep in front of the TV, and somehow sleepwalked behind Olivia's pod. But I doubt anyone would believe it was an accident. It's better, I think, to take my chances that Olivia will be fine in the morning. It was only ten seconds. I crawl into my pod and strap myself in for the night.

By 10:00 A.M., Olivia still hasn't pressed the call button. Lily raps on the lid.

"Olivia, you awake?" she says.

We gather and wait for her response, but the pod remains silent. I breathe slowly, working hard to keep my composure. Olivia's bones must have been pure liquid when I unplugged her pod.

I try to reassure myself. At least I did nothing to interfere with the ventilator, which runs on a separate power source, and the lapse was brief—ten seconds, fifteen at most. Still, fifteen seconds is an eternity at the nadir of bonelessness.

Lily presses the manual release and the lid shudders up. She shoos us back, but not before I catch a glimpse of Olivia. She is a pile of flesh without human form, rippled like caramel dripped from a spoon. Her skull forms an ellipse. One eye has rolled back in her head. The other stares straight ahead from a loose socket. The whole heap of her is wet-looking, like cheese left out to sweat in the sun. My stomach turns, and I reel back instinctively. It's the most grotesque thing I've ever seen.

Greg carries Olivia to an exam room. I go to the courtyard and sit on a bench, picking at my cuticles. My mind is fogged with terror that the others will discover my crime. I know that with each passing minute, the likelihood that I will confess diminishes. The time to do so was last night, as soon as I replaced the plug, when perhaps some of the damage to Olivia's body could have been mitigated.

Tim comes out after a few minutes and kneels beside the wildflower plot.

"Lily thinks Olivia must have missed a dose of her meds," Tim says, his back to me. "She can't talk. There might be brain damage."

"That's awful," I say, genuinely horrified. I wish he would stop talking.

"They think it's weird that she would suddenly get so much worse. She was improving."

"Who knows, with this disease?"

"It's weird, is all I'm saying." He's gathered a pile of flowers at his knee.

"What are you doing?" I say.

"We're making a garland for Olivia's pod," Tim says. "So when she comes back, she'll know we've been thinking about her."

I wonder whose idea it was. I wonder if Bradley proposed it, while they huddled in the corridor outside the Skeleton. I doubt he would have done the same for me.

Rick comes out. He takes a handful of wildflowers and sits beside me on the bench. He puts on his reading glasses and begins tying dental floss around the stems of the flowers. I consider offering to help, but I sense their project has no space for me. I go back inside, where Olivia's pod stands open like a display casket. The vinyl gleams, still slick with fluid; Greg hasn't yet had a chance to wipe it down.

Eventually, we drift back to the TV room, seeking comfort in our routine. Bradley joins us there, for the first time in weeks. He hesitates for a moment before sitting next to me on the loveseat. He glances at me with a perfunctory smile, then turns his attention to the TV.

Amy is back on *Maury* for the fourth time. This time she's brought a man in his forties with tattoos and a wet-looking ponytail. He slouches in his seat, legs splayed wide, with an attitude of profound boredom.

"Arturo, you *are* the father," Maury announces. The crowd erupts. Arturo's knee jiggles. He smiles and shrugs as if this has happened to him many times before. Bradley leaves the TV room, the studio audience clamoring in his wake.

"She's going to be okay," I say quickly, meaning Olivia— though I have no basis for this conclusion.

"Like you care," Frankie says. I'm stunned by his hostility. I hadn't realized my jealousy of Olivia was so apparent to the men. Before I can respond, Frankie gets up and follows Bradley to the courtyard to help with Olivia's garland. I watch Arturo mumble amiably through an interview. The baby is brought out and placed in his arms. He looks at it in the grim yet resolute way a man might look at a part of his roof that has caved in, necessitating expensive repairs. It is clear he will be an absent, indifferent father, but for now everyone is satisfied that the mystery has been solved.

At breakfast the next morning, Bradley says we should all go visit Olivia in the Skeleton. I point out that she won't be able to hear us in there, but the men look at me with disgust and say that isn't the point.

Lily stands before the Skeleton with a clipboard, jotting notes on Olivia's vitals. A heart rate monitor steadily beeps. The apparatus hums, red and green lights flashing. Lily slides back the panel, exposing a smoky pane of glass at the level of Olivia's head. The men take turns crouching down. They wave and speak loudly, saying they miss her and hope she'll be back with us soon. When it's my turn, Olivia's eyes regard me with calm intelligence. Fear grips my throat. It occurs to me that Olivia might have been awake when I unplugged her pod. She would not have heard me approach, due to the hum of the ventilator, but she would have felt the anti-gravity shut off and then lurch back on. It could not have been an outage; the ward's backup generators are configured to prevent even a momentary lapse. The only conclusion was that someone had unplugged her pod, and I am the only patient capable of moving in the middle of the night.

"Hi, Olivia," I say. Her eyelids slowly shutter, dismissing me. The others wander back to the TV room. I go for a walk, hoping to calm my nerves. It's a warm day, violently bright. I slowly circle the perimeter of the Bone Ward. To the east, the mountains of Custer National Forest rise in felted ridges. To the north, I can just make out the converted red barn that houses the Epidermal Ward. Beyond that, stacked on a hill, sit the low white barracks of the Hirsute Ward. I circle back to the front of the Bone Ward, which faces east. I squint down the road that runs unpaved, wheel ruts pressed into dirt, for five miles before intersecting with Highway 212, which leads to Billings. I could call a cab and escape before my crime is discovered. But I need to clear my release with Dr. Will. I need prescriptions and a plan for continued treatment. Without medication, my progress will quickly come undone.

I enter the ward, eyes aching against the sudden dark. I hear the low murmur of voices in the TV room. As I approach, the men shudder to silence.

"What?" I say.

No one will make eye contact. I know they've been talking about me.

During a commercial break, I follow Bradley to the kitchen. He flips the switch of the electric kettle.

"What's up with you guys?" I say.

"Nothing," he says.

"Come on, Bradley," I say. "What's going on?"

Bradley does not look at me. He peels the foil envelope of a tea bag.

"We were just talking about how weird it is that Olivia got so much worse all of a sudden."

My stomach folds. I nod, playing along. "It *is* strange," I say. "But relapses can happen with diseases like this."

"Dr. Will says he's never seen it."

"Well, he doesn't have a huge body of evidence to draw from, does he?"

The kettle rattles. Bradley pours water into his mug.

"Your bones are back to normal," Bradley says. "Why don't you go home?"

I watch him slowly bob the tea bag, its string coiled around two fingers, as if he has not just hurt me again.

"You want me to leave?" I say.

"I find it strange that you don't want to."

"I do want to," I say. "I'm just not strong enough, yet."

"Greg says you've been staying up later and later."

"Why were you talking about me to Greg?"

Bradley shrugs. He lifts the dripping tea bag and drops it into the trash before it's had a chance to steep.

To absolve myself, I must regress. I must mirror Olivia, becoming another patient whose progress has inexplicably reversed. I stop taking the medications doled out with breakfast. I stash the big red pills along the inner lining of my pod.

I don't expect it to happen so quickly. My bones soften earlier each night, and I wake to the old pain of bone tunneling through flesh. One night I'm watching *Dateline* after the others have gone to bed and when I stand my legs crumple under me like wet cardboard. I lie on the tile until Greg finds me on his final round through the ward. He carries the soft mass of my body to my pod. He straps me in with quick, aggressive movements, anxious to be done with me.

In the morning, I report to Dr. Will's office. Dr. Will is a lanky blond man of indeterminate age, his face eerily smooth from Botox and retinoid creams. He's based in Los Angeles, at Cedars-Sinai, but committed to a year on the ward to further his research on TNBL. Dr. Will sits on his wheeled stool, thumbing through my chart and shaking his head.

"I don't get it," he says. "You were doing so well."

I feel guilty for skewing his data. I'm sicker than I was the day I arrived, five months ago, at the Bone Ward.

"The same thing happened to Olivia, didn't it?" I say carefully.

"Yes, but Olivia's TNBL was far more advanced than yours. Her condition has always been tenuous. But you! You were almost ready for discharge."

I'm relieved that Dr. Will doesn't seem to find Olivia's relapse suspicious. I nod along to his suggestions, his proposal to double my dosage. At the end of our meeting, I'm emboldened to ask, "How's Olivia doing now, anyway?"

Dr. Will sighs and massages his temples; the subject clearly causes him grief. "Her condition is improving, but it'll be a long road. She should be out of the Skeleton soon, at least."

Fear dances up my spine. "And the damage?"

"From what I can tell, she's suffered a major setback. She won't be able to speak, at least for a while."

"How terrible," I say, exhaling.

A few days after my consultation with Dr. Will, Olivia is wheeled out for breakfast. Her eyes are dim, her mind seemingly numbed by painkillers and a triple dose of bone-girding meds. Her beauty has been chewed to a pulp: her face flattened, her lower eyelids sagging, her cheekbones fallen. Greg prepares her a smoothie in place of solid food. Olivia uses her fingers to pinch her lips around the straw.

We try to pretend everything's the same as before. Frankie says, "Hey, Starling, let's see those pearly whites." Olivia slowly raises her face. Her eyes flare with determination. She attempts to hitch the rigging of her muscles into a smile, but her mouth cants at a grotesque diagonal. Her upper lip curls to expose a single canine. The men force chuckles and murmurs of encouragement.

I can't bear to watch any more. I get up from the table and take my dish to the kitchen, exaggerating my new limp.

The next morning I wake later than everyone. Lily carefully unstraps me from the Velcro scaffold and peels the cuirass from my chest. I am too weak to stand. Greg and Lily lift me from the pod and wedge me into a wheelchair. The lights of the ward blur. I hear the clinking of forks on plates as I'm wheeled past the dining room. I can't turn my head to face them, but I know they're watching me.

The Skeleton wraps me in its purr. Needles of cold, highly pressurized air pulse into me, penetrating every millimeter of my skin. Even through the cloak of morphine, this pain is like nothing I've felt before. It is many magnitudes worse than reconstitution. It feels as though my skin has been peeled off and coarse salt rubbed into the open wound of my body. My mouth opens in a silent scream. The air is pumped with high doses of bone-girding medication, acrid clouds that sear my trachea. I remain awake, in agony, for hours that stretch into days.

Finally the Skeleton powers off. The hatch opens. Lily's face is drawn in apology.

"Okay, dear," she says. "You made it through." My eyes well with gratitude. I resolve to begin taking my medication again. Anything to avoid being sent back to the Skeleton.

Lily wheels me to the TV room. It looks to be late afternoon, the sun casting wedges of light through the west-facing windows. The men stare at me. I adopt Olivia's old tactic of diverting attention from my pain to theirs.

"How are you feeling, Olivia?" I ask. She's still in a wheelchair, her head slumped toward her left shoulder. Her lips bubble with saliva in response. The men glance at her, then avert their eyes. They seem relieved that I look the same as before, my body pumped back to recognizable form.

"Good to see you, Gumdrop," Frankie says. "You had us worried."

It's enough just to be out of the Skeleton, but it seems my plan has worked better than I'd hoped. During dinner, the men treat me like they used to, as though I have redeemed myself through suffering. Even Bradley looks at me again with fondness. I resolve to be good for the rest of my life, to make up for what I've done to Olivia.

"Nice to have you back," Bradley whispers, squeezing my hand under the table.

I begin taking my pills again. I double-dose myself, drawing from the stash I've collected in the seams of my pod. I pray my progress will be quick, but after such an alarming relapse, I know Dr. Will won't sign off on my discharge until I've been stable at least a few weeks.

My time in the Skeleton has put things into perspective. I am now eager to leave the ward, to return to New York, as any sane person would have wanted to do months ago. I am eager to sink back into the normalcy of my morning commute, of working in an office among people who don't know what I'm capable of. The ward has been restored to its proper dimensions, the grim way I perceived it when I first arrived. When Bradley's attention pivots toward me again, I resist. I do not deserve his affection, considering what it has driven me to do. I spend most of my days alone, reading in the courtyard and texting with people back home, preparing myself for reentry.

But it doesn't take much for Bradley to wear down my resistance. One day, I'm reading Dickinson in the courtyard when he comes out and joins me on the bench. I ignore him for a few minutes, then give up, putting the book down.

Bradley takes my hand. He massages the joints and presses his lips to my knuckles. "I've missed you," he says, and I know he isn't only referring to my time in the Skeleton, but also to the weeks after Olivia came, when he chose her over me.

"I've missed you, too," I say cautiously.

"I didn't appreciate what I had with you," he says. "I didn't treat you well. I'm sorry."

My skin warms. I feel my resolve crumbling. "It's okay," I say.

In an exam room, I complete my surrender. Bradley presses his body to mine. He kisses the nape of my neck. His fingers press my pelvis and thighs, molding my supple bones into the shape of his desire. I taste his skin, wishing I could unhinge my jaw and swallow him whole. As we lie entwined, my back to his, I cry silently, because I know I will never actually have him. The other times I've been in love, there was hope of a future. With Bradley, I harbor no such illusions. I have given up on the dream of a life together beyond the ward. What I feared from the beginning was confirmed the day Olivia arrived—that given a world of women to choose from, he will never, ever choose me.

Perhaps it is possible, though, to revise my idea of love. To remain in the present; to love Bradley now even though I know he will only hurt me, in the end. But it doesn't really matter either way. I am too weak not to claim every moment with him that is offered.

When it's time to leave the exam room, I wipe my eyes so he won't see I've been crying. We've waited a bit too long, and my bones are soft. Bradley picks me up and carries me to my pod. Before he lowers the lid, he pauses to kiss my forehead, as I'd told him my mother used to do, when she tucked me in for the night.

One morning, three weeks after I resumed taking my meds, the men propose we go for a hike.

They're already gathered around the breakfast table when I enter the dining room, talking in hushed voices so Lily won't hear.

"It's supposed to hit eighty this afternoon," Tim tells me, excitedly.

"Sounds nice," I say. "But what about Lily?"

"She's taking a half day," Rick says in a low voice. "Doctor's appointment in Billings."

"It's Dr. Will's day off, too," Tim says. "We won't get another chance like this."

"I dunno," I say.

"Come on, Gumdrop," Frankie says. "You used to take walks all the time."

"I'm not as strong as I used to be."

Bradley wraps his arm around my shoulders. "You should come," he says. "The vitamin D will do you good."

We pack lunches: thermoses of bone broth, kale chips, cartons of Greek yogurt. Around one, Lily comes to the TV room.

"I'll be back in the morning," she says. "Greg will be here in a few hours for the night shift. And Dr. Will is on call if anything happens."

"We're good, Lily dear," Frankie says. "Go do what you gotta do."

We stand at the entrance and watch Lily's hatchback disappear over a hump in the dirt road. For the first time in the six months I've been here, the Bone Ward is left unattended.

The sun is hot on my shoulders. We walk toward the base of the foothills, Frankie and Tim forging ahead, Bradley and me picking our way slowly over the scrub. Rick waddles alone between the two groups, sun searing his bald patch.

We walk for over an hour.

"Bradley," I say, my breath coming short. "I need to rest."

We sit beside a juniper bush. Bradley has carried our lunches in a backpack. We drink water and bone broth. We share a Tupperware of limp kale chips. When we're done eating we lie back and gaze into the dome of the sky.

The other men circle back, settle in beside us, and eat their own lunches. No one seems in any rush to return to the ward.

"Shouldn't we be heading back?" I say.

"In a minute," Bradley says.

"We want to watch the sunset," Frankie says.

I've lost track of time. When Frankie mentions the sunset, I sit up, alarmed, and see that the sun has begun its descent toward the mountains. My skin prickles with awareness. Once the sun is down, it will be too late. In another half hour my bones will be too weak to stand on.

"No," I say. "We have to go now."

"You go on ahead," Tim says.

"We're watching the sunset," Rick adds. Their voices are mechanical, as though they are reading from a script. I realize they must have planned this for weeks. Perhaps Olivia confirmed their suspicions while I was in the Skeleton. Maybe she has learned to communicate through taps of her fingers, through saliva bubbles or blinks.

I rise to my feet, my body trembling. I try to run, but my legs buckle under me after two steps.

"Poor Gumdrop," Frankie says. "You should have remembered to take your pills." I look at him, stunned; I realize how easily they could have found my stash of pills, those long days I was locked in the Skeleton.

The men get up. They stretch and yawn. So this is how it will happen—casually, their faces masked with benign smiles. They will murder me by walking away.

Bradley stands over me. I grasp his ankle with both hands.

"Please, Bradley," I say. "I love you."

"I'm sorry," Bradley says, "but you did this to yourself."

The sun melts into the jagged line of the mountains. I watch the men limp back to the ward. I try to crawl after them, but my body feels weighted by wet sand. My flesh sinks into the earth. My bladder wrings out its contents. Above me the sky grows cluttered with stars. The ward's windows are stark squares of light in the deepening gloom. Greg will arrive soon and begin making his rounds, strapping the men into their pods. I dare to hope he will notice I'm missing. But the men have probably planned this part, too. They'll simply close my pod's lid and tell Greg they've already tucked me in for the night. I'm angry only at myself, for being so naïve.

Coyotes wail in the distance. Soon they will find me and sink their teeth into my boneless flesh. I pray that my bones will reconstitute inside them at sunrise, piercing their organs, killing them. My eyes sparkle with their own starlight and I know I'm about to pass out from the pressure on my brain. I comfort myself with unlikely scenarios. Maybe the coyotes will be repulsed by the smell of my excretions. Maybe my bones will form again in just the right way, skull not slicing through brain, ribs not lancing heart. I survived many nights, after all, before coming to the Bone Ward.

The coyotes howl closer now. The wind raises whorls of dirt, filling my open mouth with tiny stones. My lungs suck against themselves. My heart struggles to fill its chambers. Darkness, silence, a pit without walls. Into the void of the boneless night, I fall.

Doe Eyes

get this idea that I'll go out into the woods and get shot. That'll show those men, the hunters. They'll be put off killing for good, if they shoot a woman in the heart. Though to be honest I'm hoping it won't be my heart. Ideal would be a flesh wound from which I can easily recover. I'll lie on a narrow bed at Mercy hooked to chirping machines. The hunters will come and beg my forgiveness. More important, my husband will visit and beg me to come home. *Your brush with death has put everything into perspective,* he'll say. *I want you back, baby. Forgive me.* He'll take me to the house on Gilbert and nurse me to health, feed me spoonfuls of Sprite with the bubbles stirred out. He'll change my bandages and whisper that he loves only me.

I'm living with Dad on the old homestead, a ranch house

in the countryside north of our university town. It's October, the start of deer-hunting season. Sunday morning I cook Dad breakfast. I toast his bagel how he likes it, four rounds until it's a puck of ash that I smear with peanut butter. The char must remind him somehow of his rustic and impoverished Ozarkian youth.

Dad crunches his bagel. I eat plain yogurt straight from the tub and stare into the yard. The dining room opens, via sliding glass door, to the patio, a patch of concrete bordered by ruined marigold plots and the clothesline where my mother used to hang her cotton nightdresses; spring days, I'd watch their white bellies distend in the breeze. On the concrete Dad has sprinkled dried corn for the deer, but this morning they don't come. Earlier, we heard gunshots. Now I spot orange flashes through the trees.

"They're awful close to the house," I say.

"Who?" Dad says, startled by me, as usual. He's already opened his thousand-page volume of Nazi war tactics. All day he'll hunch over the tome, jotting symbols in the margins.

"The hunters," I say. "They were here yesterday, too. Haven't they killed enough?"

"Hunters hunt," Dad says, his voice like a shrug. "That's the way of things." He turns to his book and is lost to me. Dad's a history professor at the state university in town. He teaches a popular class on WWII. He's writing his third book about Stalingrad. No surprise he doesn't care about murdered deer. His tolerance for death is uncommonly high.

I wash our plates and put on a deerish outfit. Brown corduroy pants I bought at Goodwill to paint in, when my husband and I moved into the house on Gilbert. A brown sweater of unknown provenance. For all I know it has existed in the bottom drawer of this dresser from the beginning of time.

I slink out to the woods. Wet earth slurps my sneakers. The hunters are in the meadow, a dad and his teenage son. I crouch behind a tree. They crouch too, waiting for something to move so they can kill it.

I went with my husband to a shooting range once. It was in a strip mall. You handed over your ID at a counter, filled out paperwork, put on earmuffs and goggles. In a narrow booth my husband stood behind me, wrapped his arms around me, showed me how to shoot. The gun was heavy and cold. I was wearing a pink shirt. I thought I'd feel powerful with a cold, heavy gun in my hands. But instead I felt bored. I knew I'd be a terrible shot, and that the point was to perform my incompetence in a charming way. I wanted this initiation to be over so we could eat lunch. I fired at paper cut into the shape of a man. My husband guided my hands to the kill.

He wasn't my husband yet. We were still just dating. From the gun range we went to Taco Bell and split a dozen hardshell tacos. We ate them in the car, which was a police car, because my husband is a cop. It was one of the things we eventually disagreed about, his being a cop. But at first I kind of liked it.

I wonder what my husband would say if he saw me out in the woods trying to get shot. Get the fuck out of the woods, is what he'd probably say.

The hunters' backs are to me now. I rustle some leaves in a way I hope is deerlike, but they're too far to hear. I give up and slink back home, disappointed and relieved. Their truck is parked on the gravel that forms a cul-de-sac in front of our house. I wait for them in the living room, watching deer videos on YouTube. I practice my deer gait on the carpet. At dusk they return. The grown hunter carries a doe slung around his shoulders. Her pink tongue lolls. A yellow tag dangles from her left ear. First murdered, then tarted up with cheap jewelry.

When we were dating, I asked my husband, over text, what he liked about me. *Your big beautiful dough eyes,* he wrote. I pointed out his misspelling. He was a sport about it. It became one of our running jokes. My husband says he's dyslexic, by which I think he means that he doesn't much like to read.

I study the regulations on the website of the Department of Natural Resources. I learn that it's legal to shoot crows only from October 15 to November 30. For two days in October the youths get first crack at the rooster pheasants, which have presumably grown sluggish and overconfident in the off-season. I learn there is continuous open season on groundhogs and pigeons. I learn that the euphemism for killing is "harvesting."

Monday, I go to the sporting goods store. I peruse a rack of marked-down camouflage. I choose pants and a jacket in clashing forest prints. At the gun counter I ask to see their best shotgun. The young worker brings it from the safe. He gives me the rundown. Twelve gauge, satin walnut, nickel-plated.

"It's Italian," he says. "A Benelli." He lets me hold it. I run my fingers over the stock. His eyes glaze with desire. "I want that gun in the worst way," he says.

For dinner, I make venison burgers. Dad's reading another

Nazi book. He pauses to ask if it's beef, this meat already in his mouth. "Venison," I say. "Deer," I clarify. He nods as if a puzzle piece has fallen into place.

I go out after dinner to break in the camo. I get down on all fours. I lie on my stomach and roll across the frozen dirt, getting twigs and leaves in my hair. I curl my body around the trunk of a tree. I'm all alone in the forest. I miss my dumb husband, the cop.

November ends. I hope my husband will call on my birthday, at least send a text. But the day shudders into focus, dissolves without a word. By rights I should be the one to forget him. He was the one who wrecked us. I sat on the couch in our living room and asked if he planned to keep seeing her. The way he said yes, as plainly as if I'd asked if he'd eaten already, if he'd slept okay, if he loved his mother, Judy. He didn't want a divorce, he said. But he had to see for himself. See what? I asked, and he shrugged.

At this point in the season, it's only legal to kill deer with bows. Through the living room window, I watch the hunter and his son park on the cul-de-sac and get out of the truck carrying guns. I could report their violation to the DNR. I could use this as an excuse to contact my husband. I could call him like I would an acquaintance from college. Hey, I'd say, my voice incidental, a draft from a door left ajar. I thought you might know something about this.

But we're on county land, beyond my husband's jurisdiction. He'd say to call the sheriff, if he answered at all.

I follow the hunters outside. I hide behind my usual tree.

A cluster of deer stand ten yards to my left, velvet snouts in the soil. The hunters crouch at the lip of the meadow. The boy aims. His moment has come.

The boy shoots, and the deer scatter. He's missed. I leap from my hiding place, utilizing all my deer talents. The forest goes silent. The hunters walk toward me, faces puzzling me out.

"The heck are you doing?" the dad says. "You're gonna get yourself killed."

Up close, he's handsome in a lush and disconcerting way, like a retired soap star.

I have no answer for him. I trot back to the house.

Shotgun deer season begins. Statewide, all the hunters turn out for opening day. On the ridge behind our house, four of them stand overlooking the creek. I wear my mismatched camo. I stroll along the dry creek bed that marks the boundary of Dad's property. They shout at me to go away. I shrug, say I live here, this is our land. There's nothing they can do. They move along the ridge to escape me.

The season will end in just a few weeks, on December 22. My window is closing. I seek out hunting hotspots. I figure it's only a matter of time, a certain density of hunters, before a stray bullet finds me. I locate a makeshift range off the road to Amana. Men and boys shoot paper targets pinned to bales of hay. I linger at the fringe. I edge beyond a line painted in dirt. They look at me and I leave.

I post an ad on Craigslist under "gigs." I write that I'm a PhD student. *I'm looking for a hunter who uses a muzzle-*

loader or shotgun to harvest small game, I write. *I'm conducting a survey to further my inquiry of masculinity in the American Midwest. I will pay each participant $20.*

I get five responses. Saturday afternoon, I rent a room at the Hampton Inn off I-80. I schedule half-hour appointments back-to-back.

Four respondents are in their forties and seem to badly need both the twenty dollars and someone to talk to. The fifth is twenty-two and thinks he's going to get laid. I've created a survey, for verisimilitude. I ask the men questions about their mothers. I ask how much meat they consume in a typical week. I ask if they've ever fantasized about shooting a person.

"Not killing them," I say. "Just a flesh wound."

One by one, the older men shake their heads. "Well, maybe my ex-wife," one says, then spends five minutes equivocating.

The twenty-two-year-old says that yes, he thinks about it. "Could be cool," he says. My pulse quickens. We face each other in chairs. He's wearing a camo jacket, jeans, Timberlands, and a khaki-colored snapback. All the men came dressed in full hunting gear.

"Would you shoot a woman?" I ask.

"Sure," he says. "What difference would that make?"

I unfurl a hypothetical. Say this woman wanted someone to shoot her. She longed to feel a bullet pierce her skin. He'd be in no danger of prosecution. He would drive her to the hospital after. She would say she'd been walking in the woods and was clipped by a bullet from pheasant hunters who were too far away to even know they'd shot her.

The boy nods. "Sounds kinky," he says.

This is an odd, promising reaction. I put away my legal pad, on which I've been scrawling pointless notes on the psychological interiors of these men. I hand the boy a twenty-dollar bill for the survey. I say I'll give him eighty dollars more after he shoots me. Fear flickers in his eyes and I worry I've transitioned too abruptly from the hypothetical. But then he says sure, he just has to be on campus by six for a trig study group.

We drive two cars to my house, the boy following me in his dusty black truck. I stand in the meadow on a raft of trampled barbed wire. Dusk veils the woods. I shiver in my wool coat. I hope the boy's hands won't be too numb to shoot. In another ten minutes it will be too dark to aim. The boy raises his gun. He peers through the sight.

"In the arm, right?"

"Or the shoulder. Just clip me."

He stands ten feet from me. His hands tremble around his gun. I close my eyes, breathe the smoke-tinged air. My mind empties. I surrender. I imagine lying in the hospital with my fresh bullet wound. My husband will rush to my bedside, ashamed of his prior indifference. He'll demand to know what man did this to me.

I hear boots crunching hay. I open my eyes. The boy is leaving.

"Hey," I say. "What the hell?"

"I can't do it," he says.

I follow him, offer him money I don't have. My bid goes up to two, three hundred.

He shakes his head. "No offense, lady, but I think you might need professional help."

———

I've run out of options. I decide to go straight to the source. My husband always sleeps with his Glock on the nightstand. He's never fired it in the line of duty, but I imagine he wouldn't hesitate to do so in the event of a home invasion. He would shoot to protect his girlfriend, the twenty-four-year-old nurse.

Late one night, I drive into town, to our old house on Gilbert. I wear black jeans and a black turtleneck. I park in the alley and pull a ski mask over my face. I approach the back of the house. I find a good-sized rock in the garden I planted two springs ago. I regard the windows, considering which one to shatter.

The back door opens. My husband holds a full white garbage bag. He's wearing a gray T-shirt, basketball shorts, rubber Adidas sandals. He looks at me, crouched in the garden. Slowly, I stand.

"What are you doing here?" he says. He knows it's me, even with the ski mask. That's how marriage goes.

I stand there holding my rock. I have imagined this moment for six months. There are so many things I want to say to him. He comes down the steps, walks twenty feet to the alley, puts their garbage in the can for collection, then turns back to the house. He pauses again at the door. We look at each other. I let the rock fall.

The next morning I linger in bed. Dad chars his own bagel. The air's warmed. Snow melts in gray mounds like piles of laundry. Corn molds on the patio, its luster gone.

I think about how my husband looked at me before latching the screen door. It was the backwards glance you give a car you've just parked. There it is, you think.

I bet he didn't even tell the nurse about me when he went back to bed. I stood still and deer-silent for several minutes, listening for my own echo.

Dad knocks on my door. "You hungry?" he says. I don't answer. He's too timid to enter uninvited, still traumatized by my volatile youth. I roll over twice more, hoping there's sleep left in me.

At eleven I go to the living room. I boot up Dad's PC, log in to my email. The young hunter's written, *I'll do it for $500.*

I reply that I don't have that kind of money.

I roll onto the carpet and do some core exercises. Dad comes in and sits on an ottoman. He peers down at me. Now I know how those books feel.

"Look," he says. "Are you okay?"

"I'm fine," I say. I make a big show of counting my crunches. Dad goes away.

A new email pings. I kneel on the swivel chair. *Forget the money*, the young hunter has written. *I've got a bet going. I'll cut you in for half. You game?*

I drive to the reservoir. The young hunter's waiting in the picnic area with two friends. They're slightly different flavors of the same human being, the only variables hair color and hue of plaid. They're all wearing down vests and drinking forties of Budweiser. The hunter offers me one from a cooler and I take it because it seems to mean something to them. They must have bought an extra, just for me.

"You really trying to get shot?" says the boy with the darkest hair.

I shrug. "I've sort of lost interest," I say. They all look disappointed.

"You don't have to do anything you don't want to do," the blond boy says.

"I'm pre-med," says the dark-haired boy. "I can tend the wound. As long as it's superficial."

"It will be," says the hunter. "I told you, I'm a good shot."

"But you don't have to do anything you don't want to do," the blond boy repeats.

I feel light-headed. I feel like some new variety of pervert. I take a swig off my forty, say I just want to talk. We sit on a picnic table. I ask the boys about the girls they've fucked, the girls they wish they could fuck, the girls they've really loved and the ones who have hurt them. They all claim to have known heartbreak, but the details are superficial, the delivery void of affect. Carefully rehearsed stories that help them to score.

The sun is low. It's cold again and I zip up my jacket and stand. The boys stand, too.

"I'm going home," I say.

"Okay," the blond boy says, stretching the word out.

"You sure?" the hunter says. "I'm a really good shot."

I think, what the hell?

"Make it quick," I say, and the boys spring to action. They lead me to the spillway wall, show me how to stand, arms and legs splayed like a gingerbread woman. They ask if I want a blindfold. I say sure. The blond boy produces a yellow bandana from his back pocket. He folds it carefully, then ties it gently over my eyes. I listen to the wind, to the thrum of distant cars on the interstate. It's Christmas Eve, I remember. I wonder if Dad even knows. After this, the boys will probably go straight to their families' homes. They'll eat ham and distribute poorly wrapped gifts, items purchased last-minute from Walgreens. They won't mention just having shot a woman. It's nobody's business but ours.

"You ready?" one of them says.

I say yes before realizing he wasn't talking to me.

The House's Beating Heart

We discovered the house's beating heart after Margaret poured the dregs of her papier-mâché project down the kitchen drain. The rest of us were in our bedrooms on the second floor, slogging through graduate coursework, when the thumping began. With each beat, the floorboards throbbed. The thin walls trembled, paint sloughing off in broad flakes.

We traced the beat to a locked closet in the kitchen. The house contained dozens of such locked closets and cabinets. We had assumed the landlord was storing his stuff, and the rent was too cheap for us to complain. He wasn't around to be complained to, anyway. We mailed our rent checks to a P.O. box in Greece.

Next to the sink was a drawer of loose keys. Kelly worked

her way through them, wedging keys into the closet's lock until the door opened and there was the heart, a small red boulder. Its surface was soft and raw-looking, twitching faintly in the kitchen light. We stared awestruck for two seconds, until the heart convulsed, tissue slapping the closet's back wall, and Kelly shrieked and slammed the door shut.

Clearly the clog was affecting the heart, making its beating more labored. We called a plumber. He knelt before the sink and began unscrewing things, shimmying his pipe snake, clearing newspaper slurry from the house's arteries. As he worked, the sound faded until we could only perceive the heartbeat by placing our palms and ears against the yellowed wallpaper of the closet's exterior. The plumber was not overly curious, and we did not mention the heart. As he gathered his tools, he warned us to be careful with the drains. An old house like this. Another increase in pressure, he said, could burst the pipes.

We would have been okay if it had just been the heart. Just the heart would've been kind of charming.

A week later, Teresa baked cookies. She baked to distract herself from writing her thesis proposal, something about metalinguistics—not my field. She went upstairs and distracted herself with the internet and forgot the cookies until the smoke alarm went off. I opened the oven; smoke billowed out. The house began coughing, spasms like quick, violent earthquakes. The floor rolled in waves, the house cleaving from its foundations. We clung to doorframes, shooing smoke with our hands.

When the smoke cleared, we located the lungs. Thin purplish bladders, like delicate tropical fish, stretched behind the north and south walls.

I didn't feel like planning interviews for my ethnography on a group of Mennonite women who made transgressive quilts, so I went to the attic to look for the brain. I pried up a dusty floorboard, exposing a patch of twitching pink-gray tissue. I poked it with the tip of my crowbar and received a mild electric shock. It was a fuzzy, pleasant sensation. I poked the brain four more times, then stumbled, drooling, back down the stairs.

Kelly had reached an impasse in her dissertation, a Marxist analysis of sentient kitchen appliances in twentieth-century film and literature. She found the liver in the crawl space under the stairs, and went in there to nap, her body stretched against the liver's leathery brown-red side. She would emerge hours later smelling sweetly, sourly of blood and bile.

Margaret found the esophagus at the end of the upstairs hallway, behind a cabinet door sealed with many layers of white paint. She made a sandwich, a triple-decker ham and turkey with everything. She dropped the sandwich down the dark, slippery tube. We found the sandwich in the backyard a few hours later, partially digested, the tomato slice perfectly intact.

We wondered where the house's mouth was. We wondered where were its stomach, bowels, kidneys, and other things.

The house suffered under our curiosity. One by one the upstairs bedrooms turned gangrenous. First the affected room would grow cold as a meat locker. Then the walls would become gray and crumbly. The smell, that distinctive battle-field stench, was unbearable.

We sealed the rotting rooms. We slept together on the living room floor, close to the house's beating heart.

In November we were all put on academic probation. We blamed the house. No wonder we couldn't focus, with these gigantic organs throbbing around us day and night.

We went to war against the house. We hacked off a piece of the liver and fried it with onions. It was tough as shoes, bitter as dandelion stems. We dumped nails down the esophagus. We sank our arms elbows-deep in the brain and churned it like a vat of scrambled eggs. The lights failed, the heat failed, the skeleton of the house lurched, threatening to splinter apart.

We broke into the heart closet and attacked the mound of red tissue with steak knives. The heart kept beating, hemorrhaging gallons of blood. We were covered in blood, slippery with blood. The linoleum sagged under the weight of the blood. The floor collapsed. We fell into the basement, straight into the stomach, which sealed itself around us, pinching shut like a dumpling.

We tried to claw our way out, but the stomach was strong. We writhed as the acid ate our skin. As our muscles dissolved, we peered through the membrane at the basement's repository of organs: kidneys the size of steamer trunks, the long, rippled colon, coiled lengths of intestine the color of bubble gum.

Though we'd left it tumbling from the closet in ragged chunks, the heart beat on. The heart kept beating after our bones were pulverized and excreted into the abandoned yard. The heart kept beating after the ground thawed and our bonemeal fertilized the soil, nourishing weeds that grew to the height of a man's shoulder. Slowly the house healed itself, and by August, just in time for fall semester, it was ready for new tenants.

A Scale Model of Gull Point

am the last survivor of the Gull Point Needle, an observation tower that looms fifty-six stories above the ruined city of Gull Point. From the top of the Needle I'm able to spectate on what remains of the tourist enclave, built from landfill stitched to Florida's Gulf Coast. I live in what was once an upscale revolving restaurant called the Haystack, a name chosen for the cloying slogan printed on the napkins and placemats—*You've found the Haystack in the Needle!* The restaurant no longer turns and the floor-to-ceiling windows have been shattered by bullets. Running water prevails, though who knows for how much longer. By my accounting, six of the Haystack's captives are missing and fourteen confirmed dead—from premature escape attempts, heart attack, helicopter fire. You'll find our corpses piled in the walk-in fridge.

———

My name is Shelly (Shel) VanRybroek, née Donagan. I'm a sculptor, though I haven't done much of note since grad school. I've exhibited in Brooklyn, Tempe, and a few group shows in Chicago. My CV stops short in 2011, when I became a public school art teacher on the insistence of my husband, Roland (Rod) VanRybroek. I don't blame Rod for my failure as an artist. I probably would have come to the same decision without his influence, and his relative wealth allows me to live in luxury despite my schoolteacher's salary, enjoying organic produce, imported cosmetics, and the brick colonial in Wheaton, Illinois, that I've decorated with works commissioned from my successful artist friends.

My meal at the Haystack was gratis, part of the package I'd won in a sweepstakes hosted by Sandy Soles LLC, engineers of the Gull Point tragedy. The sweepstakes appeared as a pop-up ad on my browser, while I was shopping for dry-erase markers for the upcoming school year. I'd heard stories about Gull Point since I was a kid. It always seemed like something from a dream, quasi-legal and chaotic—a peninsular land mass, physically attached to the United States, that was nonetheless sovereign territory, operated by a Maltese company, and thus exempt from U.S. laws and regulations. It was a place people went to party and fuck, gaudy but basically harmless—a slightly wilder Vegas. But recently the media had uncovered the depths of its depravity, and I imagine the sweepstakes were part of a larger campaign to woo tourists back to its fold. I thought I was lucky to win, the same rush I'd once felt upon hitting a slots jackpot in Reno, but now I wonder if the odds were much better than I first assumed.

Rod refused to come on the trip, citing the likelihood of a coup. He referenced the recent *New York Times* exposé, which I'd also read. I knew the people of Gull Point had suffered for decades and that I would have blood on my hands if I came. But I'd never won a contest like this before, and I resolved to go no matter what, to prove I still possessed some spark of defiance, some lust for risk-taking. I'm fifteen years younger than Rod. I'm an artist, or at least I was one when he met me. If he wanted an obedient wife, he should have chosen one of the female administrators at his firm, who uniformly worship him.

The conditions in Gull Point were worse than I'd bargained for. The hotel and restaurant workers had gone on strike the week before, and these establishments were currently staffed with scabs from Tampa. I crossed a picket line when I arrived at my hotel, a crowd of workers parting to allow the taxi's slow passage. They pounded on the windows, insistent yet gentle, which made me feel worse. "What are you doing here?" a young woman asked me through the glass, with genuine confusion, just before we reached the police barricade that cordoned off the porte cochère. An explosion rattled the building's facade while I was checking in; the worker behind the front desk saw me flinch, and apologized. "Fireworks," she said, unconvincingly.

Since the establishment of Gull Point, Sandy Soles had culled its workforce from people without other options: those buried by medical and student loan debt, sex offenders, and the formerly incarcerated. Now these castoffs had settled down together and started families in Gull Point, and the new generation worked the souvenir stands, with dull eyes and sores on their skin. I shuddered as I passed them on my afternoon walk. I despised the other tourists, the mostly white mainlanders in khaki shorts and logo T-shirts, availing themselves of the cheap bottles of premium liquor sold by street vendors. I considered cutting my trip short. But I felt I had earned my respite. If I'd arrived in hell, at least I had the privilege of leaving after two days and three nights, unlike the people who toiled here. I even entertained a fantasy of spreading the truth about Gull Point to people back home. Naïvely, I imagined the trip would inspire me to make art, after a long period of dormancy. I would turn out to be right, though not in quite the way I hoped.

That evening I journeyed to the Haystack, where Sandy Soles had pre-purchased my dinner as part of the prize package. In retrospect it was a bad idea to dine at the top of a skyscraper in the midst of civil unrest. When I boarded the elevator, I was simply glad to escape the clamor of explosives on the streets. As with most of the restaurants in Gull Point, the Haystack's regular employees were striking. The new workers from the mainland were doing their best, but it was obvious they didn't know the restaurant well. Service was slow, and other diners around me began to complain. A cold foreboding settled in my stomach. I watched the woman who'd taken my order huddling with the host near the kitchen doors, looking at their phones.

The lights cut out around 9:00 P.M., while I was finishing my entrée of roast chicken. The electric motor that turned the observation deck lost power, and the restaurant coasted to stillness. My table stopped in a north-facing position, perched over the city. I watched the lights of Gull Point flicker off in bands a few blocks wide until the entire thumb-like promontory was blacked out and indistinguishable from the ocean. Servers rushed to our tables with battery-powered tea lights. The manager sent around complimentary desserts, to placate us, and because the ice cream would melt soon anyway.

Rod called and relayed what was happening; he was watching events unfold on CNN. Tourists had been taken hostage in the rooms of the Landover Hotel, where I was staying. Emergency evacuations were under way, primarily by sea, as the rebels had blockaded the roads leading east, back to Florida. The uprising appeared to have been meticulously planned and coordinated, just as Rod had feared. "I told you it was a bad time," he said. My mouth had gone dry, and I wished in that moment that my husband were a different kind of person. I hurried to end the call, saying I needed to save my battery. It was the last time I would speak to him before service was lost.

I swallowed my fear with the ice cream. The other diners grew hushed, gathering near the windows to watch fires bloom on the dark city grid. One by one, the hulking white cruise ships blasted their horns and pulled out of the harbor. Of course none of us wanted to spend the night in the Haystack, but the manager insisted we were safer here than on the ground. We were persuaded by the sight of the boardwalk's Ferris wheel and roller coaster in flames, and by the muted drumming of automatic gunfire on the streets of Gull Point. Several staff members stacked tables and chairs against the stairwell door, a defensive move that seemed more symbolic than functional.

Hours passed. At one point a large, red-faced man approached the server who was stationed by the stairwell, and demanded he be allowed to leave. The server shrugged and told him to go ahead. The red-faced man gazed at the furniture barricade for a moment before slinking back to his wife. At that point our options were clear. We could stay in the Haystack, or take our chances on the streets. We overturned the remaining tables to fashion private sleeping forts. The windows were soldered shut, and without AC the heat quickly became unbearable. Among the captives was a group of four elderly widows who'd come from an Alaska-bound cruise. One of them died that first night, her body overwhelmed by heat and stress. Her name was Bonnie Neville, and her corpse can be found in the lobby, wrapped in a shroud of tablecloths. In the morning, two of the men volunteered to carry her down fifty-six flights of stairs. They returned twenty minutes later, chests heaving from the climb, and told us about the vicious firefight raging just outside the lobby. They'd hurried back to avoid being spotted.

In spite of these developments, we were in good spirits the first morning. Even the other old women took Bonnie's death in stride, explaining that they'd only met her a few days ago, on the ship. We assumed it wouldn't take long for some authority to intervene and restore order to Gull Point. In the meantime the chef prepared a massive brunch, and we gorged ourselves on everything that would spoil without refrigeration: plates of braised calamari, shrimp Caesar salad, filet mignon, smoked salmon. We drank warm gin and flat tonic and lay in squares of sunlight on the carpet. I got drunk and attempted to flirt with a married surfer named Dustin, who politely brushed me off.

By evening we had digested and sobered, and a vocal con-

tingent began discussing plans to escape the Needle. Five survivors departed at midnight. Four were college students
from, I think, the University of Indiana. The fifth was a
server named Jesse Chamberlain. We never saw the students
again. In the morning I woke to screams; Jesse's corpse had
been skewered, belly-up, on the spire of a neighboring skyscraper.

No one talked about leaving after that. We were subdued
now, resigned to wait and hope for rescue. Besides, we felt
lucky to be in the Haystack. From our vantage we were able
to witness, using a pair of binoculars that belonged to the
restaurant, anarchic scenes unfolding on the streets of Gull
Point. We saw tourists tied to lampposts. We saw young workers smashing the windows of the souvenir factories that had
long extorted their labor. We saw men emerge from one of
the hotels wearing gas masks and, moments later, a corner of
the building erupting in flames. I imagined a gang of revo-
lutionaries climbing the stairs, breaking down the stairwell
door and slaughtering us, the Needle's stem filling with
blood. We were relieved the third morning to find Jesse's
corpse gone; it must have rotted in the heat until it fell off the
spire like meat from a bone.

With nothing else to do, I turned, at long last, to my art.
On the third day, I snuck into the kitchen, seeking material
to sculpt with as an alternative to waiting idly for death. I
found five economy-sized boxes of foil and four boxes of
toothpicks, which I brought to the unoccupied southern bank
of the restaurant. I began by crafting foil likenesses of myself and Dustin, of the elderly widows, the manager, the college kids, and the restaurant staff. From there I moved to
constructing the Needle itself. My model's observation deck

measured one foot in diameter and for an entire afternoon I assembled the stem that would hold it aloft, four feet from the ground. Others came and watched me as if I were a street artist working for tips. They loudly doubted the structural soundness of my foil Needle, but I bolstered the stem with toothpicks and it stayed upright as I carefully populated the observation deck's interior space with foil furniture and figurines corresponding to each of us. This impressed everyone, and I was able to recruit two of the widows, Melanie and Rebecca, as assistants. They were happy, like me, to have something to do, to avoid thinking about how our stay in the Needle would end. I showed them how to plait the foil into tough braids, how to hide seams and smooth edges until the figures appeared cast from liquid metal. When I expanded my project to encompass the city of Gull Point, I invited the women to look out the northern windows and choose a neighborhood they wished to render.

Rebecca and Melanie were among the casualties of the seventh night. When the helicopter hovered before the north-facing windows, everyone thought it was the National Guard, come at last to liberate the Haystack. I remained crouched with the foil while the others stood in front of the windows, in the blinding floodlight, raising their arms and waving napkins—whether as flags of surrender or symbols of celebration, I don't know. It was horrible. I remember Melanie saying, "Why aren't they doing anything?" and then the helicopter opened fire, killing eight outright and mortally wounding four more.

With that it was down to me, Dustin, and a line cook named Anthony. We spent the night in the kitchen, weeping and arguing and drinking reserves of liquor we found in a

locked cabinet. In the morning the men dragged all twelve
bodies to the walk-in fridge. We expected the helicopter to
swoop back at any moment, but it never did, and we cautiously returned to the main room to savor the fresh air cours-
ing in through bullet holes.

Late that night, Dustin crouched beside my sleeping fort.
He was drunk, and he promised to do everything in his power
to give me the best possible chance of survival. It was an odd
speech, inappropriately familiar; maybe I'd become a proxy
for his wife or one of his daughters. When I woke the next
morning Dustin and Anthony were gone. Since then another
week or two has passed. I no longer keep track of days. That
about catches us up.

I wake each morning in a panic that I'm back in Wheaton,
and am coaxed to reality by the itch of carpet, the smell of
smoke from the burning city, and the sparkle of sunlight on
my vast foil model. My project now fills half the restaurant,
extending from the south windows to the stairwell door.
Within the cityscape, I've begun constructing vignettes using
a larger scale, scenes placed under a magnifier. I rendered the
souvenir factory inside which laborers were forced, on threat
of imprisonment or of having their children taken as wards
of the state, to work fourteen-hour days, using hot-glue guns
to affix tiny seashells to velvet-lined jewelry boxes. I rendered the brothels where tourists paid third-world rates for
sex with the young locals, and slightly higher rates for sex
with minors—a practice vehemently denied by city officials,
but corroborated by multiple undercover investigations. I
have planned models of the Grand Casino and the drug ba-

zaar and the complex subterranean network of T-shirt sweat-shops.

Each morning I stroll the perimeter, assessing what needs to be done. Today I pause over a dogfight. I squat carefully, my toes wedged into the gaps of Gull Point's broad avenues. I adjust the ears of one of the long-snouted dogs, which are both in mid-lunge, their hind paws planted to the ground with a paste I made from flour and water. I'm dissatisfied by the expression worn by one of the dogfighting men. He is less finely wrought than the other figures, his thin body listing to one side. I pluck him from the vignette. This is one of the figures I'll work on today, molding the face into a mask of exultant cruelty.

I've set up a worktable on the east side of the restaurant, where the light is good, the windows offering an unremarkable view of mainland suburbs across the wide, murky bay. I have requisitioned useful items from the purses of murdered women: tweezers, nail clippers, clear nail polish, dental floss, reading glasses. I work for hours without a break. I reshape the half-dozen figures I've extracted from completed scenes, and then begin crafting a new vignette in which a woman lies on her stomach across a motel bed. Above her, two amateur surgeons hover, preparing to remove one of her kidneys for sale on an overseas black market.

I finish near evening. I carefully transport the scene to its appropriate position on the model, corresponding to the strip of cut-rate motels along the northern rim of Gull Point. Once I'm satisfied with its placement I go to the women's restroom to pee and refill my water glass. I turn the sink handle and the faucet gurgles. A few drops fall from the pipes, and then only a gush of air.

I remember, with shame, that in the early days I had wasted liters of water to bathe myself, or to splash my face when I felt hot. Above me, the skylight is coated in ash from weeks of perpetual fire, and now admits only a dingy, sepulchral light. In the mirror my face is smeared with ash and oil, the muscles around my mouth and eyes slack from disuse. My gray tank top is mottled with grease, ragged at the hem where I've torn out threads for use in my sculpture. The bones of my chest protrude and my shoulders are red and peeling from working all day in a patch of sunlight. I feel, proudly, like a wild animal that has survived against the odds by tucking itself into the eaves of a crumbling edifice.

I anticipated the loss of running water, but it's still disturbing, a reminder that my stay in the Needle will soon end. I check each sink in the women's and men's rooms, and they all emit the same gurgling death rattle. My stomach lurches when I realize I'll have to check the kitchen sink, too. I haven't entered the kitchen since the walk-in was repurposed as a crypt. I brace myself, hold my breath, run in and turn the handle. Again a bubble of pressure bursts, releasing a few sun-warmed drops that I catch in my palm. A fur of human decay gathers on my skin. I run back to the main room and stand at one of the broken windows, cleansing my lungs and pores with fresh air. When my heart rate has slowed I take stock of my remaining water. On our second day in the Haystack, we'd filled every receptacle, anticipating the water supply would soon be cut. I still have two gallon-sized jugs, three two-liter bottles, assorted pots and saucepans filled to the brim, and half a dozen cans of soda. Plenty of water, enough to last several weeks if I'm careful.

The sun is setting and I bring my dinner to a table along

the west-facing windows. With the tip of a spoon I peel back the lid of the hundred-ounce can of garbanzos I opened last night. As I shovel beans into my mouth, I feel a tingling sensation, the awareness of a negative presence, and I realize it's because the town has gone silent. For weeks the battle raged in the streets as the National Guard subdued the citizens, loaded them onto armored trucks and school buses, and removed them from Gull Point. Others I saw executed on the spot. There were explosions, sirens, and the constant percussion of shooting. It was like the sound of a TV in the background, a veil of noise that made me feel less alone. But now, nothing. When did it stop? I scan my binoculars over the city. The streets are empty. The fires have been extinguished and the smoke has cleared. Gull Point appears to have been completely purged, leaving only the husks of buildings, the avenues strewn with garbage and shell casings and glass. I search for movement on the ground until the sun slips beneath the curve of the ocean and it's too dark to see.

For the first time since the men left, I panic. Events outside the Needle seem to have accelerated, reached their climax, and entered an eerie interlude, all while I was absorbed in creating a model of the town as it once existed. I think of Rod, and am flooded with guilt and a tenderness I had neglected to nurture, having reduced my husband to an obstacle to my happiness. But in reality, I was the obstacle, Rod merely an excuse. I succumbed to the comfort of his provincial attitudes, his contentment in watching TV shows together each night after eating the food we had cooked. As the years pass he's grown more insecure about our age difference. He's embarked on drastic diets and juice cleanses that make him miserable. Last fall he assembled a CrossFit gym in our basement, sculpting his body in an attempt to ward off the advances of hallucinatory younger men. He's always wielded a coarse masculinity to hide his fear that I'll slip from his grasp, and now it's happened anyway.

Until the very last moment, he hoped I would come to my senses and agree not to take the trip. I kissed him in the car, at the curb outside the Delta terminal, and said there was still time for him to change his mind—I'd booked two tickets just in case, it was part of the prize package. He shook his head and said it was too late, he hadn't taken time off work. My resentment melted away, and I was disappointed that he wasn't coming with me, sad to think that he might have been willing, had I pressed harder. I wondered if my quick acceptance had wounded him, if he expected me to insist, and if my failure to do so had exposed the distance between us. Looking back, I wish I'd been better prepared, in that moment, to render myself vulnerable to Rod—to say all the things I've been leaving unsaid.

But had I revealed myself in that moment, it's possible he would have come with me, and that would have been a disaster. He would have died quickly, venturing out with the first group in a clumsy demonstration of control. Or he would have stayed, and prevented me from creating anything of value.

Now I worry I've missed my chance to escape. Maybe there's no one out there anymore looking for survivors. I resolve to leave the Needle in the morning, before my odds diminish further. I wish I could document what I've done here, with my model, but my phone is long dead. Anyway, I can re-create it back in Wheaton. It's time to go home and account for what remains of my life. This decision comforts me as I fall asleep, in a nest of tablecloths, listening to the foil rustle as it settles into its form.

But in the morning I look over my sculpture and am struck by how much remains to be done. The northern skyline is missing several key buildings, and the boardwalk attractions could use reshaping. Many sections now appear sloppy and ill conceived, especially those I created early on, when I was less experienced with the medium of foil. Daylight has scattered my melancholy. I now feel only urgency to finish the project. I will push it as close to perfection as I can manage, even if I'm the only one who will ever see it. I know how fleeting inspiration can be. I'm afraid to squander this momentum and never recover it.

I lose track of hours. In the afternoon I hear, and feel in my chest, a dull, distant thudding, and look out in time to see one of the brick factory buildings shudder, the wall that faces me caving in like the face of a rotting pumpkin. The city is no longer empty. While I was preoccupied with my model, cranes and bulldozers and excavators have been dispatched to Gull Point and now riddle the landscape like a herd of yellow animals. The city is being chewed up and broken down. The loss of running water must signal the next phase of the project. Once everything on the surface has been razed, the Sandy Soles corporation will begin tearing into the city's subterranean infrastructure, prying up buried pipes and wires until no future archaeologist can unearth evidence of the crimes committed here.

———

Within a week the boardwalk has vanished: the rides and game kiosks, the overpriced seafood restaurants and high-rise hotels. Then the casinos and factories are leveled, and the spoked configurations of Sandy Soles employee housing, and finally the government buildings that always seemed tongue-in-cheek, as if behind the ostentatious faux-marble facades one might find only a civic-themed brothel.

I ration my water carefully—three cups a day, taken in tiny sips at measured intervals. I keep telling myself, one more day, one more scene, and I'll leave. But with each vignette, I have ideas for five more. Besides, the journey home terrifies me. I will have to walk ten miles south, to the checkpoint, and explain why it's taken me so long to evacuate. At first they'll suspect I'm an enemy of the state, one of the rebels disguised as a lost tourist. Even after I've established my identity, I don't know how I'll be allowed to board a plane; I'm filthy and practically naked. Perhaps I'll be given some sort of refugee garb—a souvenir sweatshirt, ill-fitting khakis. Rod will pick me up at O'Hare and we'll go home and eat a meal prepared in accordance with his Paleo diet, maybe hunks of chicken wrapped in raw cabbage leaves, a perverse simulacrum of tacos. My husband will insist on making love, to demonstrate his gladness that I've survived. After, I'll go to the garden shed that doubles as my studio and stare helplessly at projects I will never finish, that mean nothing to me.

I dread every step of this process. So I stay in the Needle, and my model becomes more elaborate and more difficult to tear myself away from. On a parallel track, the city beneath me is destroyed, block by block, a wave of destruction churning methodically south toward the Needle.

156 · Kate Folk

———

Finally one morning I stand at the north-facing windows and look down at the combed gray skull of Gull Point's absence. Behind me stretches a perfect scale model of a city that no longer exists. I am finally satisfied. It's time to go home.

I'm gathering my meager possessions—leather handbag containing wallet, house keys, phone, magnetic keycard to my room in the extinct Landover Hotel—when I hear a rumble of footsteps in the stairwell beneath me. I freeze, stooped over, one hand still groping inside my purse. I could hide in the bathroom. I could go into the kitchen, crawl in with the corpses and wait for the intruders to leave. But they are too close, coming too fast. Before I can move, the door is thrust open, easily toppling my blockade of chairs. A soldier enters in combat uniform, flanked by a team of six or eight identical men, and behind them a petite woman in her forties, wearing an expensive-looking gray suit. The soldiers see me and raise their pistols. They push the woman behind them protectively, but she elbows her way to the front and begins shouting at me. "Who are you? What are you doing in here?" She pauses, then says, "What on earth is that horrible smell?"

Two of the men force me to the ground. They wrench my arms from under my body and pull them behind my back. Electric pain shoots through the muscles of my chest. The handcuffs' chilly teeth scrape my wrists. The other soldiers fan out into the restaurant, guns drawn, while the woman demands to know who I am and why I'm here. I know the words I should say, the ones that will calm them, make them treat me civilly and shepherd me back to the living world.

But these words catch in my throat, flaring and sputtering like wet matches. One of the men has his fingers wrapped in my hair and is pressing the side of my head into the carpet. I watch their feet—the men in tan combat boots, the woman in black velvet flats—stepping all over my sculpture, flattening the figures, having not noticed a thing. In the moments before I lose consciousness, I wish only that I could be allowed to render this final scene, what I now know was always the nucleus of my model, its secret heart hidden from me until the end.

Dating a Somnambulist

One night your boyfriend sleepwalks to the kitchen and brings a handful of M&M's back to bed. You wake to bleary chocolate splotches on the sheets. You're annoyed because they're your nicest sheets. Your boyfriend says he'll buy a replacement set with a similarly high thread count. This makes you feel better. It's kind of cute, after all, that your boyfriend eats M&M's in his sleep.

Each morning you wake to a new object. A pinecone. A snow globe. A plastic lawn goose.

On the fifth night, something soft and warm tickles your calves. In your fumbling dream-state, you think it's the black cat you had as a child. Her name was Midnight and she liked to hang out under the covers. You lift the sheet to pet Midnight, but the furry mass turns out to be the raccoon you've seen rooting through bins in the trash atrium. The raccoon bites your finger, then scurries into the closet.

While you wait in the emergency room for a tetanus shot, your boyfriend agrees to go to a sleep clinic.

The clinic is blue-walled, piped through with piano music. The doctor is a small, nervous man with white hair and wide dewy eyes. He asks your boyfriend pointed questions about his somnambulism, a fancy word for doing weird shit in your sleep. He prescribes your boyfriend drugs to deepen his slumber. You're both in good spirits on the drive home. You hope the drugs will fix everything.

The next morning, the sleep clinic doctor is nestled in bed between you and your boyfriend. The doctor is bound and gagged, his moist blue eyes blinking up at you. Your boyfriend must have sleepwalked to the car, sleep-driven to the doctor's house, and sleep-kidnapped the doctor. Presumably he first had to sleep-look-up the doctor's address.

Your boyfriend allows you to shackle him to the bed frame with handcuffs, but he winds up sleep-picking the lock with an unfolded paper clip like Linda Hamilton in *Terminator 2: Judgment Day*. On the seventh morning, you wake to a brand-new microwave. From the receipt taped to its side, you learn that your boyfriend sleep-drove to the twenty-four-hour Walmart and sleep-chose the model of microwave that would best suit your needs. You're still disturbed, but pleased that you now have an easy way to heat up leftovers.

On the eighth morning, you wake hugging a famous urn from the Asian Art Museum. You've seen pictures of this urn on the sides of buses. You are worried about the criminal implications of a sleep-museum-burglary and suggest that your boyfriend stay at his own tiny, windowless apartment until his somnambulism settles down. Your boyfriend admits that he started renting it out on Airbnb, since he's always at your place anyway. A middle-aged German couple is presently staying there. Additional European couples have booked the apartment through July.

On the ninth morning, the bed appears empty. You and your boyfriend celebrate by heating frozen mini quiches in the new microwave. But when you make the bed, you discover, tangled in the sheets, a highly venomous box jellyfish native to the tropical Indo-Pacific. Your boyfriend puts on yellow rubber gloves, removes the dead jellyfish, and feeds it into the garbage disposal.

On the tenth morning, you wake to frantic nudges from your great-aunt Renetta. You haven't seen her in fifteen years. She is disoriented and upset. You take her to dim sum, show her your city, then buy her a plane ticket back to Pennsylvania.

Your boyfriend finally remembers to pick up his sleep prescription at Walgreens, but the drugs only make his nightly acquisitions more bizarre. An airplane flight recorder, battered and corroded by seawater. The slashed silver top worn by model Gisele Bündchen in Alexander McQueen's groundbreaking spring 1998 fashion show. Three passports of Americans born on August 18, 1973.

On the fourteenth morning, you wake to a wormhole squirming at the center of your mattress. Lord knows where your boyfriend sleep-acquired a hypothetical feature of space-time, but there it is, a roiling purplish vortex the approximate diameter of a basketball. You climb out of bed, careful not to touch the wormhole's iridescent rim.

You and your boyfriend spend the rest of the day sealing

the bed and its wormhole in a wooden box. While you build the box, you drop tools and planks of wood into the wormhole. You imagine these objects will pop out in a parallel universe and prove useful to parallel versions of yourselves. You imagine your parallel self is like you, but better. She probably bakes gluten-free pastries that taste just like the real thing. She probably makes her own dresses and has a killer record collection.

You consider jumping into the wormhole and emerging in a universe where your boyfriend doesn't bring terrifying things to bed in his sleep. But the parallel boyfriend might have some other, even more upsetting defect, such as snoring, so for now you stay where you are, in a sleeping bag on the floor, waiting for your boyfriend to sleep-ferry home another object that will make you shudder at the arcane puzzle of your own existence.

Moist House

The house needed moisture. So Karl was told.

He sat in a landlord's office in a strip mall off the interstate. The landlord, Franco, was known to rent out houses that were undesirable as a result of their peculiar needs and could be had for cheap. Franco was in his forties, a thickset man with plump fingers and wide, colorless lips. He wore aviator-style glasses with gold rims, and sat behind a gray metal desk, a hulking piece of institutional furniture whose severity seeded in Karl a strange docility, a readiness to take what came.

Franco leaned back in his swivel chair, appraising Karl. "It's a very special house," he continued. "Other men have attempted to care for it, with limited and temporary success.

The house is very dry, and only the most diligent tenant can provide it all the moisture it needs."

Karl wanted to laugh. "Have you tried a humidifier?"

"It's not that kind of dryness, I'm afraid."

"I can keep the house moist."

"You say that now."

Karl shifted in his seat, noting that the office was cold. The room was empty, walls unadorned, scarred desktop bereft of computer or phone, and Karl wondered how long Franco had worked out of this space. He'd been referred here by his mother, who now lived in Argentina with her younger boyfriend, a retired soccer star who modeled in billboard ads for vitamin supplements and sweat-wicking sportswear. Karl's mother had known Franco's father in the seventies, in Berkeley, her radical days. When she and Karl last spoke on the phone, she referenced this man in the misty, oblique way she employed when recalling a former lover.

Franco had brought out a thin manila folder and was examining a document inside it. "I won't charge you rent," he said.

Karl was taken aback. "Thank you so much."

Franco snapped the folder closed. "Your gratitude is misplaced. I am hiring you to care for the house that needs moisture."

"I understand."

"I'm afraid you don't," Franco said. "I doubt you've encountered a house such as this one."

"Well, I'm eager to learn. My options are limited at the moment. I don't know what my mother told you about my . . . situation."

Franco waved his hand dismissively. "The house doesn't care about your past life. It cares only about the moisture you can provide it."

He led Karl to a supply closet. "The house is accustomed to this type of lotion," he said, hauling out a five-gallon bucket by its wire handle and placing it at Karl's feet. "It will stave off the worst of the dryness, but you must apply it many times daily." He ran his palm up his forehead, slicking back the thin hair. "In fact, you must apply the lotion almost constantly. And in the meantime you might devise new ways to keep the house moist."

Karl smiled. Now that the initial shock of Franco's temperament had dulled, he found the man's devotion to the house endearing. He reasoned that landlords were often eccentric. "How moist does the house need to be, in ideal conditions?" he asked.

"There is truly no limit." Franco told Karl he could have this first bucket of lotion for free, but would need to procure his own going forward. It would be a considerable expense, but an acceptable one, as he'd be paying no rent. Karl agreed, thinking there was no way he'd stay in the house long enough to exhaust the first bucket of lotion. He doubted he'd bother with the lotion at all. He only needed a few weeks of shelter, in order to regain his bearings and find a new job.

Karl signed the lease and shook Franco's hand. He conveyed the bucket of lotion to the passenger seat of his Subaru, securing it with the seatbelt. He was in high spirits, feeling like he'd pulled off an incredible scam. He examined the bucket more closely. *Advanced Therapy Massage Lotion*, the label read. The word "massage" roused in Karl's mind the image of youthful female bodies splayed on his bed, their backsides gleaming with the freshly applied lotion; girls like Tatiana, though of course not Tatiana herself, after what she had put him through.

The turns on Karl's GPS brought him through redwood forest, then to narrow roads etched into cliffs overlooking the sea. In a small town ten miles south of his destination, he stopped at a market for provisions. As he surveyed the prices on the dusty shelves, Karl cursed himself for not having gone to the Safeway by Franco's office. He had to be frugal with the nine hundred dollars remaining in his secret Wells Fargo account. In his shopping basket, Karl placed a two-pound sack of rice, six cans of black beans, two cans of chickpeas, and a lemon to fortify his immune system. He felt rugged and resourceful as he made these selections. The cashier, an old woman in a bulky wool sweater, offered Karl no bag. Her indifference wounded him. She was perhaps the same age as his mother. Unlike the cashier, however, his mother had refused to relinquish her beauty as she aged; in the pictures she sent over email, selfies with the soccer player while they hiked or drank juice with their beach volleyball club, she appeared toned and tan, her hair dyed the same auburn Karl had always known.

"Thank you very much," Karl told the cashier, ostentatiously. He slowly gathered the groceries in his arms, making it out to be more difficult than it was in order to spite the woman for her rudeness. Back in the Subaru, he plunged into more redwoods, careening around blind twists until the road climbed again and broke onto an open plain of grass made tawny by recent drought. One last turn, onto the narrowest road yet, a single lane of mud sprinkled with gravel. In the distance, on a plateau halfway up a knob of mountain, sat the white cottage, a cube of sugar spotlit by the sun. The road terminated in a bulb-shaped patch of dirt to the right of the house, which was where Karl parked.

Karl stepped into the brisk sea air. He walked around the house, inspecting it from all angles. It was indeed a perfect cube. Its exterior was whitewashed, like the cottages he'd seen on a trip to the Irish countryside as a teenager; he'd gone with his mother, who was studying IRA tactics with her boyfriend at the time. Its slate roof sloped gently, so that any precipitation would roll over the edge overhanging the front door. The door was painted red, like a mouth with lipstick. Karl was charmed by the house's simplicity. It was like a drawing he might have made as a child, after learning to render three-dimensional shapes.

Karl paused at the front of the house. He turned to face the ocean, and was overcome by vertigo, feeling he might tip forward and tumble over the cliff. He was struck by the desolation of the region, this house the only dwelling for miles on all sides, and he imagined he was the last person left in the world. If his enemies wished to find him here, they would have to work hard to accomplish it.

The door opened with a shucking sound, like the lid peeling from a vacuum-sealed container. The interior air of the house was thick and yeasty, forming a second skin on his face. He was glad, however, to find the room clean and sufficiently appointed. A single bed was pushed into the far corner, covered by a white quilt. A table and chair were placed beneath the south-facing window, alongside a shelving unit that housed a microwave and a mini-fridge. Karl had assumed he'd have a full kitchen, and saw he'd have no way of cooking the overpriced rice he'd bought from the hateful old hag at the market. Through a doorway in the east wall, Karl found a small bathroom with a stall shower, toilet, and sink. He stood at this wall and ran his palm down its surface, which appeared to have been freshly painted. The wall seemed fine to him, not at all dry, and again Karl felt like he'd gotten away with a crime. He almost felt guilty for taking advantage of Franco, whom he'd begun to suspect was mentally ill.

Karl brought in the groceries, along with a duffel bag containing a few changes of clothes. He sat in the chair and looked at his phone, but found he had no service. No sign of Wi-Fi in the house, either. This was a relief; even if he felt tempted, he couldn't go online and see what new lies had been spread about him. It was after 6:00 P.M. and the sun was at a forty-five-degree angle, golden light pouring through the windows, so that Karl felt enveloped by a harmless fire. He watched one patch of the north wall, upon which a trapezoid of sunlight was projected. Drops of water began to sprout and gather within the golden shape, the area surrounding it taking on a sheen of condensation. The sight unnerved Karl. Wary of mildew, he brought the single beige towel from the bathroom and wiped down the wall. Franco had gotten it wrong. If anything, the house appeared overly moist.

When the sun was gone Karl turned on the lamp beside the bed. He poured a can of beans into a ceramic bowl and microwaved it. He ate the beans with a spoon, then washed the bowl and spoon in the bathroom sink with liquid hand soap. He lay on the bed, watched a few clips of pornography he'd saved on his phone, and fell asleep holding his cock.

Karl dreamed the house was speaking to him. "Dry," it said, again and again, until it screamed the word, and he woke. It was morning. The room appeared transformed. Its formerly smooth walls were now rough and flaking. In some places, the dryness looked painfully deep, tinged red, like scraped skin. The patch above the bed, the same area he'd wiped with a towel the night before, appeared driest of all. Karl ran his palm down the cool surface, loosing a shower of white flakes that were sharp to the touch. He was alarmed by the condition of the walls, and wondered if the house was afflicted with a novel form of mold.

There was no harm, Karl reasoned, in applying lotion to the walls as Franco had advised. He brought the bucket in from the car and got to work, beginning with the spot above the bed. Karl gathered a handful of lotion and transferred it to the wall, then rubbed in the lotion using the pads of his fingers. The lotion slicked the flakes down to the wall's surface, and Karl realized he'd need to "exfoliate," a verb Caroline was fond of. He wiped the first coat off with the towel, bringing the flakes with it. He then slathered an additional coat of lotion onto the exfoliated wall, after which it appeared healthy and glowing. He recalled the serums Caroline would apply to her face before bed, and was surprised by a rush of longing for his wife, while at the time he'd found her habits tedious.

Karl stood back from the patch he had moistened, which appeared fresh and gleaming, in contrast with the dull area surrounding it. The walls' dryness now seemed obvious. Karl didn't know how he hadn't perceived it before.

He moved all the furniture to the center of the room, then brought the chair to the corner where the bed had stood, and climbed up with cupped palms full of lotion. He worked his way across the east wall, applying lotion, then rubbing with the sodden towel before applying still more lotion.

By the time Karl finished moistening the walls, it was past noon. He'd planned to drive to a café in town so he could use the Wi-Fi to search for jobs. But he saw the moistening of the house was a far greater commitment than he'd anticipated. Already, the top corner of the east wall had gone dry again. Karl shivered, troubled by the thought that Franco was not insane after all. The house needed moisture, all right.

Karl ate a late breakfast of beans, then went for a walk. The wind whipped his cheeks, and he perceived for the first time his own skin's lack of moisture, the lines around his eyes and mouth cracking as he winced into the sun. Karl was thirty-eight, and within the last year had begun to feel—not old, exactly, but no longer young. This impression had been amplified by his relationship with Tatiana, a twenty-two-year-old receptionist at the consulting firm where Karl had worked for nearly a decade. As he ascended the hill that rose behind the house, Karl's blood teemed with a familiar indignation. He had not asked for such intimacy with Tatiana. It was she who'd begun messaging him on Instagram, she who had poured out the indignities of her personal life, with particular focus on the callow young men she attempted to date. Tatiana had been the aggressor all along, Karl insisting they remain friends, for the sake of his marriage, until finally he'd given in, because he'd been raised to please women, to placate them. And it was Tatiana, in the end, who'd betrayed him to Gayle in HR, and wrecked his life.

Karl stood at the top of the hill, surveying the sea. He resolved not to think of Tatiana. It made him too angry. He would find a new job, and eventually, if he wanted one, a new wife. As he made his way back down the hill, the sight of the house somehow bolstered this ambition. There it was, resplendent in its nest of brown grass. Karl propped open the door and began rubbing the walls with a fresh coat of lotion.

That afternoon, Karl perfected his technique. He learned, through trial and error, to work the lotion into the wall slowly, rubbing in small circles until it was fully absorbed before moving on to the next patch. He found the process meditative. As he rubbed, he felt the wall warm to his touch. The house seemed to purr around him. He stood at the center of the room and closed his eyes, listening to the low vibration. When he opened his eyes the walls appeared lustrous, as though lit from within.

Soon dusk had fallen, and all he could do was settle in for another meal of beans. The same sequence repeated the next day. When he woke, Karl told himself he needed to get to town quickly, perhaps after a cursory moistening, and start looking for jobs. But as soon as he began smoothing lotion onto the walls, his desire to leave the house receded. The need for employment, for money and status, felt like an abstraction, a pointless flailing of his ego. The house's needs, meanwhile, were tangible and immediate. Karl kept telling himself, just one more wall, but he could hardly moisten one wall without moistening the wall that adjoined it. By the time he'd applied lotion to all four walls and arrived at the original one, that wall had gone dry again. So the process continued, until another day had been lost to the house.

Karl's food supplies diminished at the same rate as the lotion. On the fourth day, the bucket, which had been only halfway full to begin with, was nearly depleted. Karl roused himself to action. He lunched on the last can of beans spritzed with juice from the lemon he'd gouged open with a spoon, then drove to the café in town, purchased a small black coffee, and settled in to use the internet on his phone. On Amazon, he found the lotion Franco had given him, and was shocked to find that a single bucket cost $233. At the rate he was using it, he'd need a new bucket every week. The house's moisture needs far outstripped what he could afford.

Karl stepped onto the broad pine porch of the café, and called Franco.

"I told you the house was very dry," Franco said mildly.

"I can't afford this much lotion."

"That is not my concern."

Karl considered. He had no one to turn to. Caroline refused to speak to him. His mother was in Argentina, having sex. He knew if he called her, she'd coo and say something like "Poor Karl," but it would be obvious she was merely performing what she thought to be the minimum requirements of motherhood so that she could get off the phone and back to her glamorous life. There was no other housing in the area he could afford. "Perhaps I will devise alternative means," he said.

Franco laughed. "You are welcome to try."

With some distance from the house, Karl was appalled that he'd let four days pass without any progress in his search for employment. How had he been seduced into endless moistening, as though he were an automaton? Perhaps his trance state was the result of an odorless fume produced by the lotion. Whatever the cause, he'd behaved foolishly, and for a moment he despised the house and its interminable need for moisture. "What about the other houses you have for rent?" Karl ventured. "Maybe one of those would be a better fit."

"What's the matter?" Franco said. "It's like I said, isn't it? Four days in, and already you can't keep the house moist."

"I'm keeping the house very moist." Karl now regretted having called Franco. "I was simply curious," he said, "what other houses you have."

"You don't belong in any of the other houses. You're committed to this house."

"What happens if I don't keep the house moist?"

There was a pause on the line. "It would be better to abandon the house entirely," Franco said, "than to accept its shelter while refusing to provide the moisture it needs."

Franco's tone made Karl shiver, and he hastened to end the call. Back in the café, he ordered a bucket of the lotion from Amazon, seeing no other option. He set the delivery to a local post office; for some reason, the prospect of a stranger coming to the house unnerved him. He then checked his email, hoping for a reply from Caroline, or perhaps an apology from Tatiana, or Gayle in HR. Karl felt despondent as he reviewed his uncluttered inbox, the only new message an order confirmation for the lotion.

From the café, he returned to the market. The old woman was there again, on a stool behind the counter. "Hello!" he shouted; she flinched, glancing up from her Sudoku, and nodded.

Karl cruised the aisles, propelled by a manic desire to pamper himself, as if spending $233 on lotion had exposed his life as fundamentally stupid, and thus worthy of extravagance. Into his basket he placed organic mac and cheese, rice pilaf, instant oatmeal, English tea, and a glass bottle of whole milk from a local dairy. In the produce aisle, he selected four hard bananas, an organic pink apple, and a head of broccoli he planned to eat raw, for fiber.

As the cashier rang up his purchases, Karl's mouth twitched in anticipation of an opening. He didn't know why she should despise him. "Can I get a bag?" he said.

She didn't look up, simply added the bag charge to his bill using a button on the register, and began placing items into a paper bag.

"How's it going?" he said. "I just moved into a house ten miles north."

"Lots of rentals around here," she said. "Those Airbnbs."

"Maybe you've heard about it. It needs moisture."

The woman met his gaze. "I think I know that one."

Karl's chest fluttered with excitement. "You do?"

"Seems like every six months there's a new tenant. They never last long."

"Why's that?"

She shrugged and placed the last of his groceries in the bag, the fragile thread of her interest snapping under the pressure of his question. Still, Karl felt he'd made headway. "The thing is, the lotion is pretty expensive," he said.

"What about oil?"

"Oil," Karl repeated, in a tone of revelation. "What kind?"

The cashier led Karl to the middle aisle, where she selected bottles of coconut and olive oil. These were far more expensive, ounce for ounce, than the lotion, but they were surely more potent, and could perhaps be stretched to greater lengths. Karl brought the oils to the register, but the cashier waved away his debit card. "It's on me, honey," she said, with a wink.

Karl flinched at her kindness. He realized now who she reminded him of—a woman named Tara who'd attended his mother's feminist reading group when they lived in Berkeley. He'd spent his childhood under the group's benign gaze. As a boy he had sought their approval, growing his hair long and joining them in marches against war and patriarchal oppression. He had done everything they wanted, and they loved him until he grew into a man, at which point he learned to hate them for how they shuddered to silence when he came home from football practice during their Wednesday night meetings. Suddenly he was an intruder, their enemy. His mother continued to dote on him; she tried to draw him over to the couch, to discuss whatever text they'd been reading, which Karl would have done with enthusiasm only a year prior. But now, he saw he wasn't wanted. He began performing his masculinity for them, a grotesque parody that made him hate himself. He cut his hair short. He paused at the fridge to guzzle milk from the jug, belching into the taut silence of their disgust.

Karl shuddered at these memories. He muttered a thank-you and rushed out of the market. He drove to a hardware store he'd seen on the way into town, and in the aisles approached the first employee he saw—a plump teenage boy in a burgundy smock—and peppered him with aggressive questions about interior house painting.

By the time Karl left the hardware store, now armed with sponges, paint pans, and brushes, he'd regained his composure, and was eager to get back to the house. Upon entering, he found the walls retained little of the moisture he'd left them with. The morning calm had fractured into a sharp wind that made the house groan, heightening his sense that it was suffering, and that he was the only one who could soothe it. Around the windowpanes, he saw fissures forming, and he knew he'd have to work quickly.

He first poured some of the olive oil into a pan and applied it with a foam brush, starting at the top left corner of the east wall, as usual. The olive oil left a yellow hue, and on the west wall he switched to coconut, which was slower going, as he first had to warm cloudy chunks of the oil in his palms until they melted to a consistency that could be spread across the house. He worked steadily, hoping to rouse the house to its intoxicating hum. But this time, the house remained mute, its walls cold. By the time the sun had set, he was finished. The room smelled pleasant, vaguely tropical. He'd used only half of each jar, and again Karl was grateful to the cashier; at this rate he'd be able to moisten the house far more cheaply than if he were using the lotion. Perhaps he could even buy cooking spray and cut his moistening time significantly, simply spritzing the house's walls with Pam every few hours.

Karl washed the head of broccoli in the bathroom sink, then sat in the chair and tore florets from stem with his teeth. He finished half the head in this manner, then made a carton of mac and cheese in the microwave, which he ate while surveying the walls. They appeared greasy with the oil, which

Karl found unsettling. The oil seemed not to have penetrated through to the root of dryness, as the lotion had done. He hoped the oil would continue to be absorbed through the night.

Karl slept, and when he woke his ears were filled with a high-pitched ringing, as in the moments following a great explosion. He opened his eyes to find the east and south walls, to which he'd applied olive oil, had fissured into a spider-webbing of cracks. The west and north walls, which had received coconut oil, were in worse shape, resembling burned skin, a seeping red pocked with blisters. Karl was so shocked by the sight, he was slow to register sensation on his own body. His skin felt tight and hot, like a bad sunburn. He lifted his shirt to find the skin on his chest had fissured. His lips were crusted with dryness, and when he darted his tongue out to wet them, his bottom lip cracked, filling his mouth with the taste of blood.

Karl hobbled to the bathroom, where he filled a fresh tray with warm water and soap. In the mirror above the sink he saw that every line in his face had deepened, so that he looked suddenly twenty years older. Karl felt an itchy sensation in his crotch; he pulled down his boxers and was horrified to find blisters wreathing the base of his penis. The ringing in his ears had grown louder, making it difficult for Karl to think straight. Somehow, the condition of the walls corresponded to his skin. Karl cursed himself for using the cooking oils, to which the house seemed to be having an allergic reaction. How could he have been so stupid? The house wasn't a chicken cutlet. He suspected that only by first relieving the house of its agony would his own agony be lifted.

He began by wetting the bath towel in warm water and

gently swabbing the walls until all trace of the oils was vanquished. Eventually the towel was soiled beyond utility, so Karl removed his T-shirt, wetted it, and began pressing it to the blisters. As he worked, he spoke to the wall. "There, does that feel better?" he whispered as he soaked up the wall's fluids with the shirt. He recalled his honeymoon in Puerto Vallarta, the night Caroline had gotten food poisoning from a shrimp. How he'd carried her to bed and wiped her face with a warm washcloth. He had been tender with her, then. Over the years he'd hardened to Caroline, and now, as he cleansed the walls of the oils he had harmed them with, he could not understand why his feelings had changed.

The blisters responded to his touch, healing over even as he watched. By the time he was ready to apply the lotion, the sores had diminished to pink patches. Karl peered into his boxers, relieved to see that his own blisters had similarly healed. The ringing in his ears had dwindled to a faint whine, the house nearly restored to its neutral state. He brought the half-empty oil jars outside and pitched them, one by one, toward the sea.

In the afternoon he drove to the post office, but the new bucket of lotion had not yet arrived. He checked the tracking number on his phone, and found it would not come until the next day at the soonest. In the meantime, Karl would have to find a suitable substitute. He drove ten miles inland to a Walgreens, where he spent an hour reviewing ingredient lists on bottles of lotion, cross-referencing them with the list on the bucket, which he'd taken a photo of. After a long deliberation, he purchased several bottles of expensive unscented lotion designed for sensitive skin. When he returned to the house, he found the usual faults had formed around the windowpanes. He warmed some lotion in his hands and rubbed it into the wall.

"I know this isn't the usual kind," he said softly, "but I'm getting a shipment of the kind you like soon."

The house seemed to listen. The wall gently throbbed, pressing into his palm. Its purring intensified until it rattled Karl's teeth. He sighed, sensing he'd finally sated the house's needs. It was a difficult feat, but the difficulty only made its accomplishment more gratifying. That night he lay on the floor against the east wall, stroking the house's inner face as he drifted to sleep.

Weeks passed, and Karl became further rooted in his moistening regimen. The new bucket of lotion arrived, and he ordered several more, putting the expense on a high-interest Discover card he found in his wallet. One afternoon, in his fourth week of tenancy, Karl's arm rubbed against a patch of wall he'd just moistened, prompting him to realize he could use his entire body as a brush. He stripped off his T-shirt and boxers, both of which were addled with lotion anyway. Karl rubbed the front of his naked body across the wall. Its surface warmed more quickly than usual, and Karl felt himself harden against it.

Karl no longer fantasized about naked women in his bed, bodies gleaming with moisture. He could not spare the lotion even in his imagining. The house needed all of it, every drop.

One morning, three months after he'd arrived at the house, Karl was naked as usual, rubbing lotion across the north wall with his torso, when a knock came at the door. He crouched at the baseboard, turning to see his wife's face in the front window. The sight of her was a shock. For months she'd ignored his texts and emails. On his last night in their house in Paso Robles, he'd confessed to his affair with Tatiana, aware he had no other choice. He'd been fired, disgraced on social media by Tatiana and her friends, who claimed Karl abused his power in pursuing Tatiana, when in fact it was she who'd pursued him. He'd tried to explain this to Caroline, who remained stoic throughout. She went into their bedroom and closed the door, and in the morning, calmly told him he would have to move out.

Now, Caroline had arrived at his doorstep, and he wondered if, by some miracle, she'd decided to forgive him after all. Karl didn't know how she'd found him; in the last email he sent, he'd been vague regarding his location, assuming she wouldn't care where he'd wound up. Her eyes scanned the interior of the house. Karl followed her gaze, perceiving the room through Caroline's eyes. The space was littered with empty lotion buckets, paintbrushes, and trays, like an artist's studio. He was suddenly aware of the room's smell, thick with his body odors, his semen and sweat and oily scalp, along with the faintly gluey odor of the otherwise unscented lotion.

"Karl?" she called through the cracked window. "Are you all right?"

Karl grabbed a T-shirt from the floor. He held the wadded cloth over his genitals as he stood to face his wife. "How did you find me?"

"I spoke to your mother. She put me in touch with the landlord. An odd man." Caroline moved her face closer to the gap between window and frame, squinting at Karl as though something about him remained obscure. "Can you open the door, honey? I want to talk."

The house's humming had ceased, by which Karl knew it was displeased. He approached the window, observing Caroline more closely. Her blond hair was cut into a bob with wispy bangs, as it had been when they'd first met in college. She wore a silver windbreaker and black yoga pants with a pink band at the waistline. Her small mouth was set in determination.

"Why did you come here?" Karl said. "I thought you hated me."

"I miss you, Karl. Whatever happened with that girl—it's okay. I forgive you. I want to move on."

"I've missed you, too," Karl said, and the walls of the house lurched. Karl turned to find a fissure of dryness opening on the wall behind him.

"It's time to come back to Paso Robles," Caroline continued.

"I can't."

"Why not?"

"I can't leave the house," Karl said. "I have to keep its walls moist."

Caroline laughed. "The house will be fine."

"It won't be fine," he said. "And neither will I, if I don't apply the lotion soon."

"So put some lotion on it," Caroline said, without missing a beat. "I'll help you. Then we can go."

"I can't do it while you're here." He knew the house was

already upset by the presence of his wife, and to allow her to enter would be disastrous. "Please, Caroline. You have to leave."

"I'm not leaving you here. Karl, you're scaring me."

The doorknob rattled. Caroline was trying to force her way in. Luckily, he'd locked the door. He felt the skin on his chest tighten. A corresponding dry patch on the north wall was spreading. If the house suffered, so would he. "Go home, and I'll join you there soon," Karl said.

"Forget the house! Just leave it."

Karl shook his head. "I can't do that." He remembered all the lies he'd told women in college, to maintain their hope in his affection after he'd begun to lose interest, just in case he changed his mind, and because he didn't want them to hate him. "Actually, I won't join you soon," he admitted. "The house needs me." He turned away from Caroline and resumed rubbing lotion into the north wall.

"Karl!" he heard from behind him. "Karl, I love you. Please come home. Let me in. We can talk." The doorknob rattled more violently. Karl surrendered to the wall, which hummed at his touch. It provided a scrim of noise, muffling Caroline's pleas, until, after several hours, Karl stood back from the wall and realized she'd stopped speaking entirely. He turned, and she was gone, the window's ocean view restored. Karl exhaled, feeling a great pressure lifted. He looked out at his Subaru parked in the patch of dirt. It occurred to him that he could not recall seeing Caroline's car.

The mood of the house seemed disturbed by Caroline's visit. For several days after, its walls accepted the lotion less readily. Karl was eager to get back to their routine. He purchased five buckets of lotion, along with the market's entire stock of beans, which would enable him to remain in the house for several weeks without interruption. He'd maxed out the Discover card and begun drawing money from his 401k, which he was pleased to find would buy plenty of lotion. He kept the furniture clustered in the middle of the room, preferring to sleep on the floor, his body tucked against one wall or another.

One foggy morning, he heard his mother's voice calling to him. "Karl," she said. "What are you doing in there, honey? Poor Karl."

He turned from his work upon the south wall, and found his mother's face in the window. This sight was more shocking than Caroline's had been, and Karl doubled over, his stomach clenching. He had not seen his mother in six years. She looked more beautiful than he remembered, her skin stretched smooth over her long, regal face. She wore a pink zip-up hoodie, likely a garment made by the company her boyfriend did ads for. Her breasts appeared rather large, and Karl wondered if she'd gotten implants.

Karl approached the window transfixed, without bothering to cover himself.

"Caroline called," his mother said, seeming unfazed by his nakedness. "I came as soon as I could."

"Where's Rodrigo?"

"He had to stay in Buenos Aires to shoot a commercial."

Karl imagined stroking his mother's face. Her intelligent eyes scanned his body. "Poor Karl," she said again. "Let me in, honey. Let me take care of you."

Tears formed in Karl's eyes. He wanted it to be true, that she'd come to find him. But over his mother's shoulder, he saw only his own car. "How did you get here?"

"I walked from the town." As she said this her eyes flattened and took on a dull malevolence. "Come on, Karl. Open the door."

Karl went back to rubbing lotion into the south wall. "My little starfish," the apparition said—it was a name his mother had once called him, that he'd forgotten long ago. "My beautiful boy."

The house fiercely hummed, drowning out the specter of his mother. Her voice faded, and after a few hours Karl allowed himself to check the window and confirm she was gone.

Fall edged toward winter. The fog thickened to rain. As the outer world grew wetter, the house's interior dryness persisted. In November the ceiling began to flake. Karl invested in a ladder, which he placed in the center of the room. The ceiling became part of his moistening regimen. Next, Karl realized the floor, too, needed moisture. Of course it did.

Two months passed without another visitor. Karl hoped there would be no others, that he and the house would be allowed to live together in peace. But then, one rainy afternoon, Tatiana appeared in the window.

He had turned for more lotion and caught a glimpse of darkness, which was Tatiana's form blotting out the watery daylight. She was wet, her white T-shirt soaked through to expose a black bra. Mascara streaked her round cheeks, and she wore a placid expression that seemed full of patient malice. Karl was shaken by the sight of her, though he attempted to conceal this reaction.

"Go ahead and ignore me," Tatiana jeered through the window. "You're good at that."

Karl did not respond. He kept rubbing lotion into the wall, his heart pounding.

"Do you remember the morning we woke up at your house?" Tatiana said. "You told me you loved me. Then on Monday you ignored me again."

Karl did remember that Sunday morning, but he couldn't recall saying those words. He thought he'd been more careful than that, though obviously not careful enough. Caroline had been at a realtor's convention in Stockton that weekend. Saturday night, he and Tatiana had cooked dinner together: salmon filets, a Greek salad, two bottles of white wine. They had taken a bath. He spent several hours, Sunday afternoon, working to ensure he'd washed all trace of her from the house before his wife's return.

"You made me think I was crazy," Tatiana said. "Like I imagined all of it."

"What was I supposed to do?" Karl said mechanically, without turning from the wall. "I told you from the start that it could never become more than what it was."

"I let you off easy," Tatiana said.

At this, Karl's rage boiled over. He walked to the door and placed his hand on the knob before realizing what he was doing. He glanced at the window to find Tatiana watching him, sly as a cat. "You let me off easy, all right," he said. "You ruined my life."

"Let me in, Karl," she said, her lips curling into a smile. "I'll make it up to you."

"You're trying to trick me."

"I thought we were friends, Karl."

"I was your friend. You were the one who betrayed me."

"I was angry," she said. "I was hurt."

Mention of hurt feelings stalled Karl's anger. For a moment, he pitied her. He remembered the shock of her allegation, which his boss had awkwardly paraphrased over the phone. Karl had been stunned to hear himself described as a predator. In those first terrible days, he had attempted to contact Tatiana, hoping she'd admit it was all a lie, that she'd slandered him because she felt rejected when he cut her off, citing the need to preserve his marriage. But she'd blocked him everywhere.

Now was his chance. "You wanted it, didn't you?" Karl asked.

"Of course I did," Tatiana said. "I love you, Karl."

At these words, Karl's body flooded with a warm relief, until he realized the house had stopped humming. He backed away from the window, appalled by his weakness. This was not the real Tatiana. The house was testing his devotion. He'd dispatched his wife and mother easily, but this time, he'd nearly capitulated.

"Go away," he said.

"Let me in, Karl." Her voice was plaintive now. "I'm cold. I'm all alone out here. The sun's going down."

She began to weep, which would once have made Karl nauseous with guilt. In the past, he'd say anything to stop a woman from crying, especially if he was the cause of her distress. But now, he had the house. On behalf of their bond, he renounced all sympathies that tied him to the world. He ignored Tatiana, continuing his work upon the south wall.

Tatiana proved more stubborn than the others. She remained in the window through the night, begging Karl to let her in. "Please, Karl," she mewled. "I'm so cold and hungry. Don't leave me out here all alone." Karl caressed the house back to a hum, and he hummed along with it. Together, they drowned out the sound of Tatiana's pleas. Near dawn—delirious, throat ragged—Karl emerged from his moistening trance to find that her voice had ceased. He opened the door and stepped into the gray, filling his lungs with fog. He had reckoned with the specter of Tatiana, and now she was gone, and he was free.

Months passed and there were no more visitors. Karl knew he had proven himself. He was alone with the house that needed moisture. No—the house that was always moist, now that he was its partner.

On an April day, five years after he'd come to the house, Karl lost his footing on the ladder. He had been moistening for ten hours. He'd long subsisted on a single can of beans per day, and his bones were brittle. The top step of the ladder was slick with gobs of lotion he had dropped in his moistening zeal. His hands were slippery with lotion, too, and could not break his fall.

He landed hard. Some part of his spine was broken. He was still alive, and might have recovered had he received medical treatment. But he could not reach his phone, which he'd powered down long ago and left in the Subaru, a relic of his past life. Karl watched a gash of dryness spread down the center of his abdomen, corresponding to the wound opening across the east wall of the house. The pain was annihilating, yet Karl's only regret was that in the end, he had not been able to provide the house with the moisture it needed.

Months passed before Franco registered dryness on his own skin, and ventured out to the house. He had taken Karl's silence, over the years, as a positive sign. He'd been happy for Karl and the house, which had been so particular in choosing its mate. Franco knew what he would find when he opened the door, yet he recoiled from the sight. Karl's desiccated corpse lay curled in the center of the room, next to the ladder from which he had fallen. The sun's golden light played across the many lotion buckets and dirty brushes and scraps of rotten food. A salted breeze pushed at Franco's back as he inspected the walls of the house, which appeared fresh as the day they'd been painted. They were unblemished, perfectly moist.

The Turkey Rumble

On the drive to his parents' house in Sonoma, Ruben tells me about his family's Thanksgiving tradition, the Turkey Rumble. It's like Secret Santa, he says, except instead of gifts, his family members surprise each other with minor injuries.

"Oh really?" I say, neutrally. We're halfway across the Golden Gate Bridge, which heightens my sense of peril. Ruben and I have only been dating six months, but I'd like it to last. I've never found it so easy to be around someone, day after day. Ruben is an extrovert. He loves activities. Previously, I only dated brooding nerds like myself. It's like my life was a dark room and Ruben opened the blinds, set out flowers, lit some sage, and all that.

Ruben has told me how his family is full of adrenaline junkies. His parents were once meth addicts, but they got clean before Ruben was born and started a lucrative real estate business. Now they seek thrills in extreme sports, carb-free diets, and the artful application of pain.

"It's a rush, for real," Ruben says. "Both inflicting and receiving."

"I don't really want to assault anyone in your family," I say. My gaze drifts toward Alcatraz, the boats in the Sausalito Harbor, before they disappear behind the hills. "That sounds really awkward."

"Trust me," Ruben says, putting his hand on my knee. "It'll be more awkward if you don't participate."

Ruben describes previous years' Turkey Rumbles: When he was fifteen, his grandmother pushed him down the basement stairs. Another year, his Uncle Skip soaped a washcloth and mashed it into Ruben's eyes. Two years ago, Ruben's sister-in-law Cindy heated a lighter under the table, then pressed its searing mouth into Ruben's bare calf.

"I know it's weird," Ruben says, "but it's our tradition, Zach. Do it for me, okay? Everyone's so excited to meet you."

I don't want to commit either way. I'll have to meet these freaks first. "They don't mind that I'm a guy?" I ask, tapping an alternate vein of fear.

Ruben laughs. "I've been out since I was thirteen. Don't be so corn-fed."

I'm relieved to hear this, but a little annoyed by Ruben's elitism. He never fails to point out the beauty and cultural progressiveness of California, as if he feels entitled to take at least partial credit. It's true I'm from Iowa, but I've lived here eight years, long enough to feel like I belong, if it weren't for Ruben constantly calling my attention to things like I'm a tourist.

For instance. We've exited the interstate and are now proceeding northeast on a two-lane highway. "Behold the majestic vineyards of Sonoma," Ruben says, and I admit they're pretty, cast golden in the setting sun.

"It's already snowing in Iowa," I say, before realizing I'm playing right into Ruben's stereotype of me as some kind of sexy hick.

"Thank goodness you're with me now," Ruben says. As we make several turns and enter a gated community, I start to get what he means. I knew Ruben's parents had money, but the neighborhood catches me off guard, the widely spaced houses and immaculate lawns. Ruben parks behind two columns of cars in the driveway of an enormous Spanish revival house at the end of the cul-de-sac. Before he can ring the doorbell, his mom, Linda, opens the door and throws her arms around me. She's a tan, brittle, ropily muscled blonde. It's like being hugged by a bundle of extension cords.

"Look at you!" Linda exclaims. "Ruben said you were handsome, but I wasn't fully prepared."

Linda draws me into the house, which has the vibe of a Billabong store run by teenagers. In the living room, speakers blare the Red Hot Chili Peppers. I match each family member to Ruben's description. Uncle Skip, a bachelor who makes his living volunteering for dangerous medical experiments, perches on an ottoman, looking like someone's gone after his face with a melon baller. On the leather sofa sit Ruben's older brother, Lucas, a tattoo artist and former pro snowboarder, and his wife, Cindy, a Bikram yoga instructor decked out in Lululemon. Their teenage son, Chad, sits between them, a glowering slab of flesh whose arm is in a sling—due to something innocent like sports, I hope, rather than consensual violence.

Ruben's dad comes downstairs. He's barrel-chested and hairless, dressed in board shorts and toe shoes.

"This must be Zach," he says, walking up to me. "Call me Shane." His handshake is an act of aggression. My retinas cling to an afterimage of his brilliant white teeth.

We're late due to traffic, and the family is eager to start the Turkey Rumble. Linda brings around an Ed Hardy hat, inside which our names are written on slips of paper. I draw Ruben's name, which is a relief; it seems like the least awkward of outcomes.

Shane puts his slip in his mouth and swallows it. "Let's get this rumble started!" he shouts.

We have until 7:00 P.M. to injure our secret turkey. The point is to be sneaky and original; the turkey shouldn't see it coming. I sit on the loveseat and accept a pint glass containing four shots of espresso over ice. The family interrogates me about my workout habits. I linger over details of the single CrossFit class I took six months ago, then move on to pure lies.

I'm saved by the ding of the oven timer. We gather at the table and Uncle Skip fires up the electric carver. "You don't eat carbs, do you?" he asks me. Before I can respond, he scoops the stuffing straight into the trashcan. While he's hunched over the bird, Cindy takes a jumbo bag of frozen strawberries from the freezer and swings it at his head, making contact with his left ear. Uncle Skip reels and nearly pushes the steaming turkey off the table. Everyone cheers and applauds.

192 · Kate Folk

"We have our year's first turkey!" Shane exclaims.

I long for the carbo-loaded Thanksgivings of my youth: dinner rolls, stuffing, various potatoes. Instead there is only turkey, a platter of sashimi, sautéed vegetables, and a pitcher of green fluid that Linda explains is kale blended with beef collagen. When I reach for the pitcher, Ruben places his hand over mine and says I'd better not.

"Oh, there's no nuts in there," Linda says. Ruben has told them about my allergy, how at age nine I tasted death in the gooey interior of a PB&J. He insisted his parents gather all the nut-affiliated products into one kitchen cabinet and label the cabinet with a sign that says "Danger—Nuts."

Ruben won't let me have any of the smoothie, pointing out that the blender has held nuts in the past. I remove my hand from the pitcher, feeling simultaneously chastised and loved.

Lucas asks Chad to pass the salt, and while the boy is reaching, Lucas stomps on his socked foot with the full force of his Timberland boot. Chad curses and rubs his foot with his unslung hand.

Later, while Linda is washing dishes, Chad points out the window at a fictive deer, then punches his grandmother in the stomach. She doubles over, the air knocked from her lungs. "Good one, sweetie!" she gasps.

"She didn't see that coming!" Shane says, just as Uncle Skip sneaks up behind him and jabs a fountain pen into his forearm, hard enough to break skin.

"Just what I need," Shane says good-naturedly. "Another fucking tattoo." He cradles his forearm and regards the blood pearling up around blotched ink.

We settle back in the living room. Linda asks Cindy if

she'd like more coffee, and when she brings it she pretends to trip, spilling the hot liquid onto Cindy's chest. Cindy jumps up, peeling her Lululemon tank away from her scalded cleavage. Uncle Skip wolf-whistles, which strikes me as inappropriate. I glance at Lucas, but he's laughing at his wife's pain with the rest of them.

We listen to Sublime and watch football on the muted bigscreen TV. Around six, Shane invites Lucas to the garage to admire his new power drill. We hear Lucas's scream, muted by distance and drywall. When they return, his left hand is spooled in gauze.

With that it's down to me and Ruben, which means he's drawn my name, too. Ruben's family is quiet, waiting to see how we'll hurt each other. I would've relished this opportunity with several exes, but I have no desire to injure Ruben. Over six months, he's sheltered me from loneliness, jealousy, and trace amounts of tree nut. However, I know it would be even worse to shirk his family tradition.

On the drive here, Ruben told me about the one time in twenty years of Turkey Rumbles that a participant failed to deliver her injury. Lucas had a fiancée before Cindy, a wasplike Estonian ballerina. He brought her home for Thanksgiving, and during the rumble Uncle Skip lit her hair on fire with a gingerbread-scented candle. The flames traveled rapidly along currents of hairspray. By the time Lucas plunged his fiancée's head under the faucet, her eyebrows had singed off. She refused to finish the rumble and spent the rest of the weekend locked in a guest room, mourning the loss of her eyebrows and ordering expensive hair-growth supplements using Lucas's credit card. Within weeks, they broke off their engagement.

I don't want my relationship to be a casualty of the rumble. So I do the only thing that feels right. I cross to the kitchen, open the nut cabinet, and extract a jar of peanut-flavored whey protein. Before Ruben can stop me I've inverted the jar over my face and let the powder tumble in clumps down my throat.

Ruben holds me around the waist as my knees buckle. My blood pressure plummets; my throat cinches shut. I am lowered onto the kitchen tile. Ruben grabs the EpiPen from my messenger bag and jams it into my thigh. In the moments before I black out, I stare into his eyes, trying to make him understand that I have hurt myself in order to hurt him; that in this one act I have fulfilled both of our obligations.

I wake in a hospital bed, surrounded by Ruben's family. I peer through swollen lids at the spray-tanned ovals of their faces.

"He's awake!" Cindy says.

"He's one tough nut!" says Shane, and I know I have won their respect and their love. I have won the Turkey Rumble.

Two weeks later, Ruben proposes. I agree on the condition that we immediately elope. We are wed by Christmas, which we spend at my parents' home in rural Iowa. There, Ruben is confronted by my family's version of Secret Santa. But by the time he understands, it's too late for him to escape us.

Big Sur

Meg was attending a dinner party hosted by the tech company her ex-boyfriend Matt worked for. Around twenty people were gathered in the dimly lit back room of a farm-to-table restaurant in SoMa. Seating was assigned, and Meg was surprised she hadn't been placed next to Matt, who'd begged her to be his plus-one. His boss had insisted they bring someone, and Matt had been hard up in his search; all his friends were heavily involved with the Democratic Socialists of America, and tonight was the San Francisco chapter's monthly meeting. Meg had been positioned between a blond woman wearing a plain sack-like dress Meg recognized from the Everlane website, and a tall, freakishly attractive man named Roger. His handsomeness had a strangely anodyne, cartoonish quality, like a child's idea of a prince. He was tall, with a high forehead, a swoop of caramel-colored hair, and a full mouth tinged pink, as if he'd just eaten a cherry popsicle. When Meg found her seat, he stood and pulled back her chair, smiling with disarming warmth.

"My name is Roger," he said. "Please tell me, what is your name?"

Meg was thrown off by his formality. Also, her name was displayed on a card tented in front of her plate, and she wondered why he couldn't simply consult the card.

"I'm Meg," she said, allowing Roger to shake her hand.

"Meg," he repeated slowly, as though savoring the syllable in his mouth.

The first course was served family-style, large ceramic bowls of arugula, kale, and pomegranate arils in citrus dressing, along with baskets of whole wheat sourdough with a thick, bark-like crust. "What do you do for a living, Meg?" Roger asked, and Meg told him about her work at the eye bank, attached to a hospital south of Golden Gate Park.

"I harvest corneas from donor eyes," she said.

"The eyes of the dead," Roger said.

Meg paused, unsettled by his phrasing. "Yes, that's right," she said.

"To enable the continued sight of the living," Roger said. "That is a beautiful mission to devote one's life to."

Roger kept staring at her—staring *into* her, Meg felt. A cold hand of fear traced its way up the back of her neck. She turned to the blond woman on her right, but the woman was engaged in conversation with the man seated to her own right. Down the table, Matt sat next to another stunningly handsome man. Meg willed him to make eye contact with her, drawing upon any psychic connection they might have forged through five years of sleeping together, but he was looking into his salad, nodding at whatever the man was saying.

"Did you grow up in the Bay Area?" Meg asked Roger, desperate to shift his focus from her.

"No," Roger said, sitting back in his chair and staring into the row of votive candles placed along the center of the table like a spine. "I come from the marshlands of central Florida. My father left our family when I was a boy. I was raised by strong women—my mother and her sister, my aunt, who did their best to teach me how to be a good man. Those long afternoons, I shelled beans and shucked corn with my aunt while she told me the melancholic stories of her own youth, fog settling over the swamp beyond our porch. I learned the value of hard work from these sessions, which I now employ in my job at a local technology company."

Meg had never heard someone account for his life in such a poetic way. It was disturbing, yet moving, and she wasn't sure how to respond. "What company do you work for?" she asked.

"It has an unremarkable name you would probably not recognize," Roger said. "It is a good job, one I feel fortunate to have, but I would prefer not to talk about it."

"Okay," Meg said. "Sorry."

Roger turned to her, placing his hands, long and wax-like, on the table. "Please, Meg," he said. "You have nothing to apologize for."

Dinner was over. Meg stood with Matt outside the restaurant. She'd rushed through the survey printed on the back of her place card, giving her dining companions all fives. The survey was odd—it asked her to rate Roger and Stephanie, the blond woman, using attributes like physical attractiveness, congeniality, ease of banter, smell, and likeliness to pursue further contact. Meg felt it would be unfair to rate Stephanie poorly, since they hadn't interacted. Her feelings for Roger were more complicated. He had been, if anything, overly attentive and solicitous, but to articulate why this bothered her seemed beyond the scope of a questionnaire.

"Did you like the food?" Matt asked, pulling hard on his Juul as they walked down Folsom.

"Yeah, it was good," Meg said.

"Meg!" they heard from behind them. Meg turned to see Roger approaching. Her stomach clenched, dread mingling with the habitual excitement that accompanied a new man's attention. "I had a wonderful time speaking with you at dinner," Roger said. "Could I have your phone number so that I may contact you at a later point?"

Meg glanced at Matt, who looked amused. She considered telling Roger that this was her boyfriend. But she had alluded to being single, and she'd always hated how the only certain way to evade a man's overtures was to reference one's possession by a different man. "Sure," she said. She entered her number into Roger's phone. He beamed when she handed it back to him.

"Fantastic," he said. "I will send you a text message within the next seventy-two hours."

Roger retreated down Folsom, turning north on Sixth Street.

"That guy has real balls to do that right in front of me," Matt said. "How does he know we're not dating?"

Meg was touched by his jealousy, which felt like a vindication. "I might have mentioned I'm single," she said. "You're right, though. There's something wrong with that guy."

Roger returned to the room he shared with Steve. Their company had rented out the top floor of an SRO on Sixth and Mission. Ten of them lived on this floor, two in each room, sleeping on twin beds pushed against the walls. Roger opened his door and found Steve inside, ironing his best shirt. He had a date tonight, which was why he'd been excused from attending the dinner party.

"Did you locate this woman on a dating app?" Roger asked.

"Yes," Steve said. "On Hinge. Her name is Marisa. She is a beautiful woman! I have high hopes for our date."

"I have high hopes for you, too," Roger said, though he was sad to think that Steve might have success where Roger had failed. Success meant Steve would vanish to Big Sur, as the others had before him. Roger would soon have a new roommate, someone who looked a lot like Steve, but who was not Steve.

"How was the dinner party?" Steve asked, sitting on the edge of his bed and buttoning his shirt.

Roger sat on the edge of his own bed. "It was a wonderful dinner," Roger said. "I met many interesting people, including a woman named Meg."

Steve's eyes flared with ardor. "What a beautiful name," he said.

"She is a remarkable woman," Roger said.

"Did you secure her phone number?"

"Yes. I will send her a text message soon."

"It would be wise to wait a day or two."

"I agree," Roger said, annoyed that Steve felt the need to tell him this.

Steve stood. "I must leave for my date," he said.

"I wish you luck," Roger said.

"Thank you," Steve said. Roger stood, and they embraced.

Alone in their room, Roger lay on his bed and looked up at the ceiling, which was flaking in a pattern that reminded him of starry summer nights from his childhood. He thought about Meg and looked again at the digits she had entered into his phone, numbers corresponding to a human woman who could relieve him of his burden. His body flooded with a familiar ache.

Roger was not quite tired, so on his phone he performed one of his favorite Google image searches: "woman in hat." The grid of photos displayed women of all nationalities and of various ages, though most, Roger observed, were young. They wore many different styles of hat. Wearing the hats seemed to gratify them. A feeling of peace overtook Roger as he looked at the hatted women. He closed his eyes. He dreamed, as always, of Big Sur.

Meg saw the text on her lunch break.

Good morning ☺, the text read. *This is Roger, who sat beside you at the dinner party. How are you feeling today? Please describe your emotional state.*

Meg squinted at her phone screen. Again the eerie feeling washed through her. She was reminded of Words with Friends games she used to play with strangers who attempted to engage her in flirtatious conversation, often calling her "dear." They usually seemed to be older men from distant countries, but sometimes she suspected they were bots. She would have thought Roger was a bot, too, if she hadn't already met him in person.

I'm feeling fine, she wrote. *I'm at work.*

Roger responded immediately. *At the eye bank, where you dissect human eyeballs in exchange for an hourly wage?*

Meg wondered if he was making fun of her. *Yeah*, she wrote. *How are you?*

Roger replied with a picture of a beagle. *I have just encountered this dog in a local park*, he wrote. *I think it is very cute. Do you like dogs?*

Sure, Meg wrote.

I love dogs, Roger replied. *I love all animals. I would never hurt one deliberately.*

Meg was often amazed by how bad men in the Bay Area were at texting. She was bored by this exchange, but intrigued by the idea of fucking Roger. She had not expected him to contact her, assuming his request for her number was part of a pickup artist's regimen. He was absurdly attractive in a conventional way she'd always found repellent, assuming men who looked like him had no hope of being decent—not to mention the fact that they'd never been interested in her. Roger, though, seemed different. His childlike submissiveness hinted at a certain depravity they might enjoy together. She imagined having sex with Roger, issuing commands until she'd had her fill of him, and then telling him to leave.

So are you gonna ask me out on a date? she wrote.

A few minutes ticked by, and Meg figured she'd scared

him off. Oh well, she thought, picking at her salad. Her fingertips still smelled of the vinegar solution in which the eyes were preserved.

But then Roger's reply lit up her phone screen. *Oh, Meg, I would be honored to take you on a date. It would be my life's singular pleasure!*

Meg took a screenshot of their exchange and texted it to her roommate, Genevieve. *That freak from last night,* she captioned.

Wowww, Genevieve replied. *What a thirsty boy.*

Roger's company was headquartered in Russia, and had no physical office in San Francisco. On weekdays, Roger went to various parks and worked on his laptop, following instructions emailed each morning from his supervisor, Kirill. He drafted emails that informed people of wonderful news: they had been chosen as the recipient of a one-million-dollar inheritance, or there were many attractive people in their area who wanted to achieve sex with them. He sent these missives to the thousands of email addresses Kirill had provided. He attempted to give each email a personal touch. *Ms. Erma Clark,* he wrote. *It is my pleasure to inform that you have been named as benefactor in the will of the honorable King Olav V of Norway.* It filled him with joy, telling people their lives were about to change for the better. He was grateful to be engaged in such meaningful work, though the people to whom he sent these emails rarely responded.

Roger would work until his laptop ran out of battery. Then he would relax in the park, admiring dogs and reading the novels of Haruki Murakami. Kirill had recommended Roger read Murakami as part of a cultural enrichment program that would enable him to converse with the women he targeted. Many American women had read at least one of these books, Kirill claimed, and even if his date hadn't, Roger could still talk about them, perhaps making the woman feel insecure about her ignorance. Insecurity rendered a woman vulnerable, making her more likely to feel a trip to Big Sur was in her best interest.

Roger had perceived a new tension in his correspondence with Kirill, as the months stretched on without Roger completing his mission. He was ashamed of his failure, though he'd followed every instruction he was given. He used the dating apps diligently, swiping right on every woman, finding each of them possessed of an almost unbearable beauty. When he achieved a match, his chest surged with joy, and he began constructing a mental picture of his future with the woman on his screen, culminating with their trip to Big Sur.

But even when he was able to secure a first date, it was difficult to maintain a woman's interest beyond their initial meeting. Roger had not yet managed to achieve sex, though he felt he'd come close with a corporate lawyer named Sasha, who'd consented to see Roger three times. On their third date he had taken her to a seafood restaurant in the Castro, where he asked questions about her life until, shortly after they'd finished their entrées, she said that he was exhausting her. When the check came, Roger reached for it, but Sasha grabbed it first, placed a hundred-dollar bill in the leather folder, and fled into the night, too quick for Roger to follow. Later, she texted him an apology, saying she was under a great deal of pressure at work and did not have the "mental bandwidth" to continue seeing him, though she thought he was a very nice person and wished him the best! Roger texted her a few more times over subsequent weeks, but no quantity of careful attention could reignite her willingness to see him. He did not understand what he was doing wrong.

Roger had arranged a date with Meg for Friday night. Late Thursday, he asked Steve for advice on how to proceed without repeating the mistakes he'd made with Sasha. Steve had just returned from his second date with Marisa. He'd achieved sex with Marisa, and now Roger kneeled at his feet, helping to extract Marisa's data from his penis.

"You can't be too eager," Steve counseled.

Roger paused in his work to look up at Steve. "But it is good to be eager, isn't it?" he said, then continued gathering data from Steve's genitals using the sterile swab.

"Only once in a while," Steve said. "You have to conceal your excitement, so that in the rare moments you expose it, the woman is surprised, and works to elicit further excitement."

Roger completed the swabbing and transferred the data to a vial that Steve would mail to headquarters in the morning. He stood, and Steve put his hand on Roger's shoulder. "Thank you," he said. "I find it difficult to perform the extraction myself."

"Understandably," Roger said. "I am happy to help."

"I hope that when you achieve sex, I can return the favor."

"I would like that," Roger said, though he was starting to fear this would never happen. He felt the pressure of Steve's hand on his shoulder, and it occurred to him, in a flash of pain, that Steve didn't believe it would happen, either, and was only saying this to comfort him, out of pity.

Roger and Steve curled together on Steve's bed, Roger's arm slung across Steve's chest. He liked when it was just the two of them here, in the little room with a sink in which they took turns urinating. He knew that soon, Steve would take Marisa to Big Sur. Each roommate had gotten there more quickly than the previous one, and perhaps his next roommate would be so efficient, Roger would not even have a chance to help with the extraction.

"Let's try something," Steve whispered. "Tell me again about shelling beans with your aunt."

"I remember my aunt's stoic face as she squinted into the marsh where the alligators dwelled, recounting the beatings she endured as a child at the hands of my cruel grandfather," Roger said.

"No!" Steve said. "That's too much, Roger. Do you tell this to the women you are hoping to achieve sex with?"

"Of course," Roger said. "It is the truth of my past life."

"Don't you have any other memories?"

Roger thought for a moment. "I remember my aunt's boyfriend, who rode a motorcycle and smoked methamphetamine, and who once forced me to murder an owl that had roosted in the eaves of our porch."

"Oh dear," Steve murmured.

"I was a poor shot," Roger said, shuddering at the memory. "The owl did not perish quickly."

"Okay, what about since you've lived in San Francisco? Do you have any pleasant memories?"

Roger thought of his various roommates. How they held each other after he extracted data from their penises. But this seemed too personal; he did not want to tell Steve about the roommates who came before him, and a memory that involved Steve directly didn't seem like what Steve was asking for. He thought of the dinner party.

"I remember Meg," Roger said. "How she used the tines of a fork to remove the ice cubes from her glass of water, so they would not inflict pain on her teeth."

"Okay, that's better," Steve said.

"She placed the cubes on the tablecloth, where they melted and formed a dark patch on the linen."

"That's very good," Steve said. "Women like when you perceive small things about them."

"Should I text her immediately, recounting this memory?"

Steve paused. "Perhaps not," he said. "Remember, you can't seem too eager."

"Yes, you are right," Roger said. "I will wait to tell her in person."

Roger remained still until he knew that Steve was asleep. Then he untangled his limbs from Steve's, urinated into the sink, and returned to his own bed. He imagined Meg smiling beneath the brim of a large, soft hat.

Meg sometimes wondered, as she got ready for a date, what her mother might have told her about men if she'd had the chance. Her mom had died when Meg was seventeen, and only met one guy Meg was involved with—Josh, who'd been a senior at the town's public high school when Meg was a freshman. One Saturday, a month before her mother's cancer returned, Josh came to pick Meg up in the afternoon. He wanted to meet Meg's parents, to "do things right," he said, as if he were planning to marry her, though they didn't have much in common. Meg had never been sure if Josh really liked her, or if he was merely enjoying the idea of himself as an old-fashioned suitor. He'd worn a dress shirt and a tie, and brought Meg's mom flowers. Meg was struck by the falseness of this, how he was putting on a show of courtship, and later her mother said that he seemed nice, but a bit phony with the flowers, and how old was he exactly?

When Meg met Roger at the restaurant that Friday night, he presented her with a single heavy sunflower, three feet long and dripping, its thick stem wrapped in pink paper, and Meg thought again of what her mother would say. Meg had proposed this place, a pizzeria near her apartment in the Sunset. She assumed Roger would pay, but if he didn't, she couldn't afford to be stuck with half of an expensive bill.

"Thank you for meeting me," Roger said, when they sat down. He was wearing a gray button-down shirt, thin cotton through which Meg glimpsed the swell of his chest muscles, a faint suggestion of nipples. It was a brisk night, and she thought he must have been cold as they waited outside for their table, though Roger had shown no sign of discomfort.

"Sure," she said. "Thanks for asking."

"You look beautiful," Roger said. Meg blushed; she was embarrassed to have put so much effort into her appearance, and that the effect remained unimpressive, in her view. She was wearing one of the old dresses from the back of her closet, a cheap silk minidress that pulled tight across her chest. Beneath the dress, her black tights had quarter-sized holes around the crotch, a fact she could play off as erotic if necessary.

They discussed splitting a pizza. "Do you like Hawaiian?" Meg said.

"What is that?" Roger said.

Meg paused. "Pineapple and Canadian bacon, or ham," she said.

"I have never heard of such a pizza."

"Where did you grow up again?"

"I come from the marshlands of central Florida," Roger said.

Again Meg noted the stiltedness of Roger's diction, combined with his odd cultural blank spots. "Where are your parents from?" she pressed.

"They are also from Florida," Roger said.

"Okay," Meg said, giving up. "Well, it's a divisive pizza, but I like it. What do you like?"

Roger put down his menu and gazed into the distance. "I suppose many people would consider an ideal pizza to be topped by a form of meat and a form of vegetable. Or, if a person does not consume meat, one or two vegetables, or no topping at all."

"But I'm not asking about a hypothetical pizza ideal," Meg said. "I'm asking what *you* like."

"I have not given much thought to my preferences. I want only what makes you happy, Meg."

Meg was annoyed by Roger's refusal to participate in the decision. It reminded her of so many nights deliberating over dinner options with Matt, who would always claim to be "open to whatever." He'd seemed to think his flexibility was a magnanimous gesture, but in practice it had merely placed the full burden of deciding on Meg. The waitress approached, and Meg ordered for both of them, with an offhanded, almost arbitrary resoluteness—like a businessman, she thought. They would share a carafe of the house wine, a Caesar salad, and a large pizza, half Hawaiian, half sausage and mushroom. Roger stared at her throughout this transaction, his eyes bright with awe. His attentiveness made her uncomfortable, just as it had at the dinner party. When the waitress was gone, Meg busied herself with her napkin, spreading it and laying it across her lap, to delay meeting his gaze a few moments longer. She felt ugly and poor in her old, ill-fitting dress, juxtaposed with Roger's sleekness. He looked out of place in this family pizza restaurant, as if he were a Hollywood actor come to study the ways of regular people in preparation for a role. The huge, heavy sunflower sat on the chair next to her like a corpse.

"How was your day?" Roger asked. "Did you cut up some eyeballs of the recently deceased?"

"Yeah, it was a good night for the eye bank," she said. "Six pairs of eyes."

"That is fortunate," Roger said.

"Not really," Meg said. "It means six people died."

The salad came, and Roger served a heaping portion onto her small white plate before taking a more modest amount for himself. "Have you ever read the novels of Haruki Murakami?" he asked.

"I don't think so," Meg said.

"You should try it sometime," Roger said. "His work offers many insights into the human condition, and modern society."

Meg decided the only way out was through. She asked Roger to summarize one of the books he'd been reading, and tuned out during his rigorous synopsis. She wanted to ask him what his deal was—what was wrong with him—but didn't know how to phrase it in a way that wasn't hurtful. It was possible, she now realized, that he had suffered some trauma that kept him frozen in a childlike state, preventing him from developing social skills. This thought softened her view of him, and she felt guilty for having judged him previously simply because he was so attractive. She observed Roger as he summarized the Murakami novel, filing away data points that she could later convey to Genevieve.

Before their date, Meg had already decided she would fuck Roger tonight. It had been a while, six months or so, since she'd had sex, and she felt she had nothing to lose. Roger was hotter than any guy she'd ever slept with, and she wouldn't mind, would in some ways be grateful, if he never contacted her after. She had buzzed her pubic hair with a battery-powered trimmer she kept in her room between uses, so Genevieve wouldn't be tempted to trim her own pubes with it. She'd shaved her legs and treated the skin of her ass with a clay "butt mask" that a woman from her yoga class had given her last year as a birthday present. She wore a lacy peach thong, one of three pairs of underwear she reserved for nights on which getting laid was a possibility. She was ready, and determined that her preparations would not go to waste.

When the bill came, Meg made a pretense of reaching for her wallet, but Roger insisted on paying, which pleased her. They stood on the sidewalk, Meg clutching the sunflower in her arms. Roger proposed they take a walk in Golden Gate Park, but Meg said it was too cold; they could hang out at her apartment, if he wanted. Roger's golden-brown eyes widened.

"Are you sure, Meg? That seems like an important step."

Meg laughed, rather unkindly, she knew. "Okay," she said. "Never mind."

Roger fixed her with a serious look. "I would like nothing more than to enter your apartment," he said. "I just want to make sure it is what you want, too."

"I was the one who suggested it," Meg said.

"Yes," Roger said, nodding. "This is true."

They walked to Meg's apartment on Noriega. Genevieve was out for the night, but for once, Meg wished she were there to get a read on Roger. She usually took pains to sneak men into her room unobserved, because Genevieve tended to consider all the guys Meg dated to be losers, which bothered her only because she knew Genevieve was right.

"What a beautiful apartment," Roger said. It was not beautiful. It was low-ceilinged, carpeted, and dirty, with a cramped living room and two small bedrooms off a hallway in which the bulbs had burned out. It was hard to believe that Matt had lived there with them for two years, though it helped that he'd owned only a duffel bag's worth of clothes. Meg felt embarrassed, assuming Roger lived in a luxury condo downtown, though she figured the promise of easy sex would render her other inadequacies moot.

Meg showed Roger to her bedroom. She deposited the sunflower on her bedside table, plugged in the multicolored Christmas lights strung around her window, then sat on the bed and began taking her shoes off. Roger remained standing in the middle of the room. "Come sit," Meg said, patting the bedspread beside her.

Roger eased his weight onto the bed. Here they were. She was offering her body to him, and was curious to discover what he wanted to do with it.

Roger did nothing. "Do you want to kiss me?" she said finally.

"I would like that," Roger said. "May I?"

She nodded. He pressed his mouth to hers, dryly, and Meg was reminded of childhood afternoons she'd spent pressing the faces of two Barbie dolls together, prodding their paddle-like hands at each other's hard breasts and blank crotches.

"Put your tongue in my mouth," Meg said, and Roger did.

It was a bit like she'd imagined, yet also too strange to have imagined. Roger would not do anything without Meg's explicit instruction. She took off her dress and tights and told him to lie on his back. She straddled him and unbuttoned his shirt, exposing his hairless, muscular chest.

"I cannot believe this is happening," Roger said.

"Please stop saying that," Meg said.

She told Roger to put two fingers of one hand inside her. Meanwhile she unbuttoned his jeans, spat in her palm and gripped the base of his penis. Roger trembled. "I love you," he said.

Meg decided to pretend he hadn't said this. Roger's dick, like the rest of his body, was perfect, but something in their dynamic felt off. She was used to surrendering to the relentless forward momentum of male desire, a swell she could lose herself in, like being pulled out into the ocean. This felt like way too much work.

"What do you want me to do?" Roger asked.

"I want you to stop asking me that," Meg said. "I want you to do what you want to do."

"I want to make you happy," Roger said.

"It would make me happy if you'd fuck me like you don't care about my feelings," Meg said.

"Okay," Roger said, and proceeded to do what she asked, kind of.

When it was over, Roger cuddled up to her, resting his head on her shoulder. Meg wanted to tell him to leave, but unlike in her fantasy, she found herself incapable of meanness. "Thank you," Roger said. "That is the first time I have achieved sex."

A panicked feeling rose in Meg, as if she were about to be murdered. "Excuse me?"

"I am so happy, Meg. So happy that I could do this with you."

Meg sat up, drawing her legs to her chest. "You were a virgin?" she said. "How old are you?"

"I am a thirty-four-year-old man."

"Were you raised religious?"

"I was raised by my mother and aunt in the marshlands of central Florida."

This was exactly what he'd said before. Meg shivered. "I think you should leave," she said.

Roger sat upright, suddenly attentive. "Have I offended you, Meg?"

"No," she said. "I would just prefer to sleep alone."

"I understand," Roger said. "It can be difficult to fall asleep with a stranger beside you. And I know that is what we still are to each other, though I hope this will change in time. I hope that in the future, when we know each other better, we will be able to sleep together comfortably, our bodies touching at various points."

Roger put his clothes back on. He leaned over and kissed her cheek. "I will contact you in the morning," he said.

"If you want to," Meg said breezily, relieved he was leaving without a fight.

"I will talk to you soon," Roger said.

She waited until she heard the door shut behind him, then got up and engaged all its locks.

Roger walked back to the SRO, thrumming with awareness of Meg's data written upon his body. He flung open the door of his room. Steve lay on his bed, reading *Kafka on the Shore*. When he saw Roger, he leaped up to greet him.

"How was the date?" he exclaimed.

"It was indescribably wonderful," Roger said.

"Did you achieve sex?" Steve said, and Roger nodded, a grin spreading across his face. Steve embraced him, then got to work swabbing. They had used a condom, so Steve focused on the area around Roger's testicles. Roger offered the fingers of his right hand, the ones that had penetrated Meg's body, and Steve ran the swab along them from base to tip.

For the first time, Steve joined Roger in his bed. Steve was the one to cuddle up against Roger's back, his arm slung across Roger's chest. "I am so happy for you," Steve said.

"Perhaps I will make it to Big Sur after all," Roger said.

"Of course you will," Steve said. "I've asked Marisa to go next weekend, and she has agreed. Maybe we'll be there at the same time!"

Roger's chest clutched at the prospect of Steve's departure. "I do not think I will make it by then," he said. "I have not yet broached the subject with Meg."

"No matter," Steve said. "If not next weekend, you will join us there soon. I have faith in it."

"Oh my god," Genevieve said, laughing. "He was a *virgin*? How is that even possible?"

They were sitting at the kitchen table, eating oatmeal. The table's surface was covered in unopened mail and Genevieve's acupuncture textbooks. Meg had looked forward to recounting her night to Genevieve, but she now felt annoyed by the pleasure Genevieve was taking in the details. "I don't know," she said. "Maybe he went through some kind of trauma."

"Sure, sure," Genevieve said. "I mean, no judgment." She said this without apparent irony; Genevieve was the most judgmental person Meg had ever known. Without her usual eyeliner, Genevieve looked like a child, her round face puffy, lips swollen from sleep. She was not conventionally beautiful, but Genevieve harbored a self-assuredness that drew people to her, broken people who longed to be told how to live, and with whom Genevieve amused herself temporarily before gently breaking their hearts. She possessed the unyielding self-esteem of a person with rich parents who loved her unconditionally, who called her every Sunday evening, hoping she'd soon tire of her West Coast experiment and move back to Connecticut. Genevieve would have been capable of using Roger for sex, laughing in his face when he told her he loved her, but Meg had known too much of life to treat people so casually.

"I feel bad," Meg said. "It seems like he's really into me, for some reason."

"I have to meet this guy," Genevieve said.

"I can't see him again," Meg said. "I don't want to lead him on."

"Come on," Genevieve said. "After all I've done for you."

She said this jokingly, yet it was not a joke. Meg knew that she herself was one of the broken people Genevieve gathered around her. Genevieve had paid their full rent some months when Meg had unexpected bills, shrugging at Meg's promises to repay her. She had agreed to let Matt move in, because she'd recognized it was important to Meg, and because she lived by a personal code of never standing in the way of other people's happiness, which also meant allowing them to make their own mistakes. She could offer her guidance, her sharply honed judgments, but people were free to ignore them.

It was nine o'clock, Saturday morning. Roger had already texted: *Good morning, beautiful Meg. When will I see you again?*

Days passed, and Roger continued texting Meg. Her responses lacked enthusiasm, and whenever Roger asked when she was available to hang out again, she would say something vague about how busy she was.

"She may want to achieve sex again when the weekend arrives," Steve told Roger on Tuesday, after examining their text exchanges. "If you do not text her for several days, she will fear she has lost your affection, and contact you to discover if her suspicions are correct."

Roger saw the wisdom in Steve's thinking. He stopped texting Meg. He reflected on the details of their first encounter, in case he should get another chance to achieve sex with her. She had responded most positively when he did not speak, when he simply focused on inserting parts of his body into her orifices. She had recoiled when he told her he loved her, and Roger resolved to never do this again, though it was the truest thing he had ever known. Roger asked Steve if he would be willing to practice kissing. Steve agreed, and they spent Thursday afternoon engaged in this practice, first with Steve pretending he was Meg, then with Roger pretending he was Marisa, and then with Roger pretending he was Meg and Steve was Roger, until by the end Roger felt ready to approach kissing Meg from any perspective, including his own.

Friday night came, and Meg still hadn't texted. Roger began to despair. Steve had left on a date with Marisa; in the morning, he would return to their room to pack his things, and he and Marisa would leave for Big Sur. At 10:00 P.M., desolate in his solitude, Roger walked to Golden Gate Park. He was gazing upon the dark, shimmering surface of Stow Lake when he felt his phone vibrate in his pocket.

Meg was drinking with Genevieve and Genevieve's classmate Hugo at the Bitter End. Genevieve had insisted she tell Hugo about her date with Roger, and Meg did so reluctantly.

"Oh my god," Hugo said. "What's he doing now? Can we meet him?"

At first, Meg demurred, but then she grew drunker, and a little horny, and started to think it would be nice to have Roger come home with her again. Sexually, he presented a blank form that she could shape into whatever she wanted. He was so eager to please her. And she felt a little mean, evading his invitations to hang out again, rather than simply telling him she wasn't interested. As she sat with her friends at the bar, Meg wondered if she had not done so because she was, in fact, still interested.

"Okay, I'll invite Roger," she said, during a lull in their conversation. Genevieve and Hugo squealed. "I'm sure he's doing something else," Meg said. It was 11:00 P.M. on a Friday. To send a last-minute text, which conveyed that it had only occurred to her as an afterthought that she might desire his presence, was the kind of shit guys had pulled on her in the past. She expected Roger to do what she did in those instances—to not write back until morning, if ever.

But Roger replied within thirty seconds, saying he was on his way. Fifteen minutes later, he appeared in the bar's doorway. Once again, Meg was struck by Roger's guilelessness. He didn't seem to realize, or care, how desperate he might seem to Meg and her friends. Most guys would have killed thirty minutes on Clement Street, maybe peering into the windows of the exotic fish store, so as not to appear too available.

She stood to greet him, and Roger embraced her. He clutched her face between his hands and kissed her, plunging his tongue into her mouth with surprising deftness. Meg returned to her seat, dazed and a little aroused. Genevieve and Hugo stared, openmouthed, and she felt a tinge of satisfaction. She'd made Roger out to be a fool, but his physical presence had a certain effect, the visceral power of hotness. He wore only a white undershirt and jeans, and his skin was flushed, as if he'd just come from the gym.

"Where are you from, Roger?" Hugo asked.

"I come from the marshlands of central Florida," Roger said. "It is a region of the United States."

Meg blushed, knowing Genevieve would fixate on the strangeness of Roger's speech.

"Wow, no shit?" Genevieve said. "Florida's part of the U.S. now?"

"Yes," Roger said. "It is one of the fifty states."

Meg glared at Genevieve, regretting what she'd set into motion, but Genevieve's gaze was fixed on Roger, her lips curled in a predatory smile.

"You're very handsome," Hugo said.

"Thank you."

"Have you ever modeled?"

"No, but I am interested in any opportunities this world has to offer."

"Right on," Hugo said.

"Let's get you a drink," Meg said, and shuffled Roger out of the booth. They went to the bar, where she ordered them pints of beer.

"What were you doing before you came here?" she said.

"I was wandering through Golden Gate Park, hoping you would contact me," Roger said.

This was the answer she'd feared. Now that he was here, she felt protective of Roger. It had been cruel to invite him simply to allow her friends to make fun of him. "You want to get out of here?" she said.

Back in her room, Meg found Roger better equipped to meet her needs. She was pleased by the way he kissed her, while they were still standing in the center of the room, and then forced her down onto the bed. He gripped her body more firmly this time. He coiled his fingers into her hair, and when she asked him to, he slapped her face lightly.

They lay together in the dark. Again Meg wanted Roger to leave, though the feeling was less pronounced than before. "I have been thinking, Meg," Roger said, and she tensed.

"About what?" she said.

"I think we should take a trip to Big Sur," he said. "It would be a romantic diversion from our everyday lives. A change in scenery would deepen our connection, enabling us to see one another differently. We could spend the three-hour drive discussing the life events that have shaped us."

It seemed way too soon to propose taking a trip together. She wondered again if Roger planned to murder her.

"Let me think about it," she said.

"Yes, please consider it seriously," Roger said. He got up and began putting on his clothes.

"Where are you going?" Meg said.

"I am returning to my own place of residence, so that you can sleep soundly," Roger said.

"You don't have to," Meg said.

"I would like to stay, but I am aware this is your preference." He bent down and kissed her cheek. "Besides, my roommate is leaving in the morning, and I would like to be there to say goodbye. I will contact you by 9:00 A.M. tomorrow. If you have any wish for contact before then, please do not hesitate to yield to this desire. I will respond immediately, regardless of the hour."

Steve had showered and dressed in his favorite chambray shirt. Roger presented him with a gray cashmere scarf, which he'd bought as a parting gift.

"Thank you, Roger," Steve said, his eyes filling with tears

as he wrapped the scarf around his neck. "I will think of you on the drive, imagining I am seeing the landscape as you will see it in the near future."

Steve had packed some of his belongings into his canvas backpack. The rest, Roger would dispose of or repurpose for his own use, clearing the way for a new roommate. "I will always remember our time together in this room," Roger said.

"Yes, but soon we will be reunited, and our memories will merge," Steve said. "I believe you have found your match in Meg."

"I believe so, too," Roger said. They embraced, and then Steve was gone. Roger went to the park and waited for Meg to text him. He observed two dogs playing, taking turns chasing a rubber stick. The dogs were of equivalent size, though one possessed a shaggy coat and the other a sleek one. The fight was playful at first, but then it seemed to turn serious, the dogs growling, teeth clenched upon opposite ends of the toy. Roger's eyes brimmed with tears. He believed all dogs should be friends, and did not like to see them at odds with each other.

Meg always told herself it would be the last time with Roger, and then a few days would pass and she'd find herself texting him. He would come over and fuck her, with increasing competence, and then hold her tight in his arms, whispering about taking a trip to Big Sur.

"When will we go to Big Sur?" Roger said again one Tuesday night, and Meg groaned.

"It's so far from here," she said. "And we don't have a car."

"We can rent one," Roger said. "Oh, Meg, it will be so wonderful."

Meg had been to Big Sur once, with Matt. They'd set up their tent in a narrow slot within a sprawling campsite. The ground was muddy, the air thick with grilled meat. All night, children screamed right outside their tent.

"I'm not really into camping," she said.

"We will not need to camp," Roger said. "We will stay in a beautiful two-story cabin overlooking the sea."

This piqued Meg's interest. She wondered how Roger had access to this cabin, but she had learned that asking him practical questions about his life only yielded unsatisfying, cryptic responses. It occurred to her that Roger was embedded in a network of tech-industry privilege that she might enjoy the perks of. Matt had been similarly privileged, but abstained from indulging due to his political convictions. He'd been a hacker as a teenager in rural Oregon, a vegan anarchist who justified his current job coding for a major tech company as a means of stockpiling cash to fund hazily defined revolutionary activities. In the meantime, he and Meg had eaten bland quinoa every night. She'd fallen asleep to the faint sound of Rage Against the Machine issuing from Matt's headphones while he stayed up until 3:00 A.M., Slacking with his comrades. She had longed, in those days, for a partner who would engage with her in expensive, ecologically irresponsible activities.

"Maybe," she told Roger. "Let me check my schedule."

On her lunch break the next day, in addition to Roger's usual morning texts, Meg found a text from Genevieve: *Omg read this.* She'd sent a link to a *Chronicle* article, which detailed a new scam involving a technology that had originally been intended for use in the healthcare sector, but whose prototype had been seized by a Russian company and developed for use in an elaborate data-mining operation. Several women had reported going on dates with suspiciously attractive men, who eventually led them to Big Sur, then stole their data and vanished in a cloud of lavender-scented mist. These men, it turned out, were not human, but an advanced form of artificial intelligence, a biomorphic robot whose cells vaporized upon completing the task with which they'd been programmed. They'd been nicknamed "blots," a term left over from the acronym used by the technology's original developer.

In the hospital cafeteria, Meg skimmed through women's accounts of their blotting, feeling nauseous. The blots' tactics were vindictive, focused on destroying the woman's reputation in addition to stealing her money. *It's been the worst six months of my life,* read a quote from a woman named Alicia.

Meg shivered. All signs pointed to Roger being a blot. She navigated back to his messages. *Beautiful Meg,* he had written an hour ago. *Have you devoted any more thought to our trip to Big Sur?*

Meg ignored both Roger's and Genevieve's texts. She returned to the lab, where she crouched over an eyeball, peering through her magnifier as she worked a scalpel around the hazel iris. The work calmed her, though her body tingled with the awareness that she'd taken a fake man into her body; that Roger was some kind of sex robot, set on exploiting her. It felt, in retrospect, like an innovative new form of sexual assault. She reflected on everything he'd ever said to her, all his odd mannerisms cast in a new, sinister light. Waves of anger coursed through her, hitting up against her memories of Roger's vulnerability. Try as she might, Meg couldn't fully convince herself that he wasn't a real person, his emotions the result of coding devised by Russian programmers to manipulate her.

As she walked home that night, Meg kept her arms crossed over her chest, avoiding eye contact with any man she passed. She had the sense of narrowly escaping calamity, once again. Another week, and she'd have gone to Big Sur with Roger, and lost her tenuous grip on a respectable life. She passed by the pizza restaurant where they'd had their first date, and paused at the window. She shivered again as she watched a young couple laugh over glasses of wine.

Roger sat in his room, alone. It was Friday afternoon, but he felt too sad to go to the park. He missed Steve, but more important, he missed Meg, who had stopped replying to his texts. Kirill had also gone silent. Roger had sent him an email that morning, asking when he would receive a new roommate, but it had bounced back with an error message. Roger did not understand what was happening. He had felt on the brink of achieving his purpose, of taking Meg on a romantic excursion to Big Sur, the journey that would finally relieve him of his burden. They had grown closer, over numerous occasions of achieving sex together, and she had even said she'd check her schedule to determine when it would accommodate a trip. But now, she would not even talk to him, and as he sat in the room, the setting sun casting a rectangle of light across the brown carpet, Roger began to worry that something terrible had happened to her.

Are you okay, Meg? he wrote. *It would be a great relief if you could simply confirm your continued existence.*

Roger watched the text go through, "delivered" appearing beneath the blue bubble of his message. At that moment, someone knocked, and Roger was disoriented, thinking that his text had summoned the knock, and that Meg herself would appear at the door. But Roger reminded himself this was unlikely. His next thought was that his new roommate had finally arrived. It had been nearly two weeks since Steve's departure, by far the longest stretch Roger had spent alone in the room. He had been unbearably lonely.

Roger opened the door to find a bald man with tired eyes, the same man he had previously seen mopping the foyer of the building.

"I need you to vacate the premises by the end of the day," the man said. His tone was harsh, the way people spoke in the park when a dog had done something forbidden.

"I do not understand," Roger said. "I live in this room."

"Whatever line of work you're involved with is none of my business," the man said. "But the city's cracking down. If you're still here in the morning, I'll call the police."

Beyond the man's rounded shoulders, Roger saw that the doors of the other rooms on his floor stood open, the hallway eerily quiet. He agreed to the man's terms, then closed the door and sat on the edge of his bed. He began crying, out of confusion. After a few minutes, he regained his composure, packed his favorite things into his backpack, and ventured out into the city to find Meg.

Everyone in Meg's world was obsessed with the idea of blots. Meg avoided discussing it, horrified that she'd fallen for one. She shut down Genevieve's attempts to speculate on how the Russian company might already be utilizing her DNA, which the articles said the blots carefully retained after each sexual encounter with a human woman. It appeared the Russian company had seen the end coming, and scaled back their operations shortly before the news broke. The remaining blots had all managed to abscond to Big Sur with their dates in the preceding weeks, and vaporize. It seemed that Roger was the only blot left in the city, and Meg was the only one who knew of his continued existence.

I do not know what I have done to offend you. I would only like a chance to make it up to you, Roger had written the following Monday, when Meg checked her phone on her lunch break.

Upon leaving work, she found Roger standing by the bike racks. His clothes were rumpled, his face drawn, as if he had not slept in days. "I can't talk to you," she said, moving past him.

Roger followed a few paces behind her. "Please, Meg," he said. "I have been evicted from my room. There is no one I can turn to. I miss you so much. The pain of losing you is causing me to slowly perish, as if my internal organs are being eroded by acid."

Meg turned to face him. "Do you understand that you're not a real person?"

"What do you mean, Meg?"

"You're a blot," Meg said. "You were created to steal women's data, destroy their credit, and humiliate them on the internet. That's what you would have done to me, too, if we'd gone to Big Sur."

"I wanted to go to Big Sur as a romantic escape we could enjoy together," Roger said.

"The police are looking for you," she said. "If they catch you, they'll send you to some lab to be experimented on. You should go to Big Sur on your own."

"I cannot go there without you, Meg," Roger said.

She paused. "Why not?"

"I do not understand it either. Some things are simply not possible in this life."

"I'm sorry," Meg said. "I can't help you. Please leave me alone." She walked away quickly, turning left at the next intersection so she would not be tempted to look back and see Roger standing there, his hands empty.

Roger's credit cards no longer functioned. He still possessed two twenty-dollar bills, money he used carefully, waiting until he was faint with hunger to purchase a sale item at Safeway. During the day, he wandered the blocks surrounding Meg's workplace, moving slowly so that his body would not require more nourishment than he could afford. One day he located a public library, where he was able to charge his phone. He remembered the word Meg had called him, and performed an internet search on one of the public computers: *What is a blot?* Roger's empty stomach clenched as he read the first article that appeared. His gaze traveled above the monitor to other people gathered in the library: a beautiful young woman crouching to read the spines of some books, a beautiful older woman waiting in line to check out, a shabbily dressed man slumped into a seat against the slot where people put the books they no longer had use for. Roger felt his heart beating hard in his chest. He wondered if it could be true, that he was different from all these people—that he alone was not human.

In the men's restroom, Roger sat in a stall with his head between his knees. His vision flooded with black, then slowly drained to reveal an image of Meg, standing on the deck of the cabin in Big Sur. Roger was filled with a sense of calm. He washed his face in the sink, then patted his skin dry with a paper towel and regarded himself in the scratched mirror. He had recognized himself in the articles. And yet he also knew that he loved Meg. All he wanted was to be near her, without causing her harm.

She would be getting off work in thirty minutes. Roger made his way to the eye bank, hoping to achieve a glimpse of Meg that would sustain him through the long night.

Meg wanted to put Roger behind her. She hoped he would simply disappear, so she wouldn't have to think about the implications of having slept with a blot. In a few years, she figured, it could be a funny story to tell people over drinks. But she soon realized Roger was still following her, at a distance, as though she were the sun he orbited. While she walked to and from work, she'd see him across the street, walking parallel to her. All night, he patrolled the sidewalk across from their apartment.

Genevieve began losing patience. She came home one night while Meg was watching *Iron Chef* in the living room, and let out a shriek of frustration. "He's out there again," she said. "I hate to say it, but I'm starting to think we should call the police."

"I thought you hated cops," Meg said, pleased to point out this hypocrisy.

"I do, but this is starting to freak me out," Genevieve said. "What if he attacks one of us?"

"He won't do that," Meg said. "It's not in his design."

Genevieve went to the window and groaned. "He's out there right now," she said. Meg looked out to see Roger crouched behind the mailbox across the street. When he saw her face in the window, he straightened and waved, with what looked like timid hope.

Meg drew the blinds. "You don't want the police poking around your acupuncture practice," she said.

Genevieve's gaze drifted to her acupuncture table, lodged into the corner along with her leather valise of needles. She'd been practicing out of their apartment for the past six months, though she was still in school and was operating without a license. Meg thought there was slim chance the police would enter their apartment, much less give a shit about an unlicensed acupuncture practice while investigating a fugitive blot, but fear of their meddling seemed to work on Genevieve.

"Fine," Genevieve said, opening her laptop. "It's about time I stocked up on pepper spray."

One night, after a post-work yoga class, Meg returned home to find Roger standing at the stoop of their building. When he saw her, he hurried back across the street, crouching in his usual position behind the mailbox. The sight of his skittishness, his awareness that he was unwanted, struck a painful chord in Meg.

Genevieve had a night class, and planned to sleep at Hugo's place in the Mission. Meg coaxed Roger inside, let him shower and charge his phone. They sat at the kitchen table, eating toast with peanut butter.

"Meg, you have saved me," Roger said. "I have run out of money, and was beginning to fear I would perish."

"There must be somewhere you can go," Meg said, though even as she said this she knew it wasn't true. Roger couldn't avail himself of the city's overburdened resources; the risk of someone reporting him to the authorities was too great.

"I have read the articles, Meg. I do not know who put me here, but whoever it was, they no longer have use for me." He grabbed her hand, his eyes flaring with urgency. "I never wanted to hurt anyone," he said. "Especially not you."

"You can't help what you are," she said. "None of us can."

She allowed Roger to lie in bed with her. At 4:00 A.M., she nudged him gently and told him he had to leave before Genevieve returned. As he left she handed him all the cash from her wallet, a mere twenty-three dollars.

They repeated this sequence several times over the following week. Meg would wait until a night she knew Genevieve would be sleeping elsewhere, and then turn on the Christmas lights in her window, so that Roger would know to wait downstairs. Meg knew she was crossing a line, that Genevieve would be furious. But Genevieve didn't understand what it was like to have no one. Her parents' house in Connecticut was a warm nest she could return to whenever she wished, the plane ticket charged to their Amex. Meg would apply her jealousy of Genevieve's good fortune like a balm whenever she felt guilty about letting Roger into the apartment.

Then one night Genevieve came home unexpectedly, while Meg and Roger were sitting at the kitchen table eating toast. She froze, keys clutched like a weapon. "What is he doing here?" she said to Meg. "Get out of my apartment," she told Roger, pointing at the door, as if banishing a dog to the yard.

Roger gathered his possessions and fled. Genevieve locked the door behind him, then turned to Meg, her hands shaking. "What the fuck, Meg?"

"I thought you were staying at Hugo's."

"I didn't feel like it. Jesus. How long has this been going on?"

"I felt sorry for him. He has nowhere else to go."

"That's not your problem. And it's definitely not mine." Genevieve settled into the chair Roger had just vacated. Her expression had softened from rage to curiosity, and Meg relaxed; Genevieve probably perceived this as just another fucked-up thing Meg did against her own best interests, as traumatized people tended to. She didn't like being reduced to a specimen for Genevieve's bourgeois contemplation, but it was better than being cast onto the street alongside Roger.

"Honestly, it seems like a function of codependency," Genevieve said. "I'm worried about you. You let people walk all over you, and then beg them for more abuse."

Meg bristled. She sometimes enjoyed hearing Genevieve's theories about her behavior, honed from years of talk therapy, another advantage underwritten by her parents. Meg couldn't afford therapy, but felt she could glean some of its benefits from Genevieve. Still, this seemed like a bitchy thing to say. "What is that supposed to mean?" she said.

"Like Matt," Genevieve said. "You're such good friends with him now, and that's nice and all. But I remember what a dick he was to you."

"I had my own part in all that," Meg said. "I guess I don't have the luxury of cutting people out of my life just because they hurt my feelings a few times."

She regretted her bitter tone, but Genevieve didn't seem offended. "Okay, but this isn't just some guy hurting your feelings. Roger was literally designed to fuck you over."

"That's the point, though," Meg said. "Someone else designed him. He didn't choose to be this way."

Genevieve sighed, apparently deciding Meg was a hopeless case. "Well, if you want to keep seeing him, that's your choice. But don't bring him here again, okay? I don't want him fucking with my stuff, or stealing my DNA, or whatever creepy shit he's been programmed to do. Next time I see him on our block, I'm calling the cops."

Now informed of the threat he faced, Roger relocated to the park. He found a sheltered area between some trees, a place where people played a game with plastic discs during the day. After dark, though, it was empty. He arranged his belongings around him. The first night was very cold, and he shivered beneath the trees. Meg had warned him that he should move frequently, to avoid detection by the police, and so when he saw a light flashing between the trees, he began packing his backpack. But then he heard someone whisper his name. It was Meg!

"Hi," she said, coming over and settling onto the dirt next to him. "I brought you a blanket."

She unfolded the blanket around him, and Roger was amazed, once again, by her kindness. "I hope you have not deprived yourself of warmth, by bringing me this item," he said.

"It's an extra." Her eyes looked sad, though her mouth smiled. "I brought you some food," she said, reaching into her tote bag and bringing out a plastic container filled with grain and slivers of chicken.

"Oh, thank you, beautiful Meg."

"I forgot a fork."

"It is fine. I will use my fingers."

They sat against the tree, and Roger ate the food with his hands. When he was finished, Meg produced a snack cake from her tote bag. "I remember you liked these," she said. They had stopped at a 7-Eleven for beer one night, before Roger lost everything. He'd been drawn to the apple pie illustration on the wrapper of the snack cake. It had roused a memory of his childhood, when his mother had baked him a pie for his birthday, and they'd eaten it on the porch, just the two of them, as the sun set over the marsh. It was one of the only joyful memories Roger possessed. And now he knew it had been implanted in him, created by a programmer in some office in Moscow.

They split the pie, their fingers growing sticky from the filling. After, Meg positioned herself on top of Roger and began kissing his neck, which made him feel warm inside. She had worn a skirt, and they achieved sex without taking off their clothes.

As they lay together, visions of Big Sur flooded Roger's

mind. He attempted to dispel these images, knowing that they were only a part of his programming, but the desire was overwhelming. Roger lay still, waiting for the force of his longing to break upon him and recede.

"I should be getting home," Meg said, untangling herself from the blanket.

"Yes," Roger said. "Go home and sleep in your warm bed."

"You can use your backpack as a pillow," Meg suggested.

Roger looked at the backpack at his elbow, seeing it in a new light. "What a wonderful idea."

"I'll find you tomorrow," Meg said. She kissed his cheek, and disappeared beyond the trees.

A week passed. Each night, Meg would go to the park to find Roger in the forest near the Frisbee golf course. His cell-phone had run out of battery, but luckily, he never moved far. The light in his eyes had dimmed, though he smiled whenever she came near. She would settle at the foot of a tree with him, and watch him eat the food she had brought. They would have sex; Meg no longer bothered with condoms, as she knew Roger could not impregnate her. She would hold him, and he would murmur about Big Sur, his former enthusiasm ceding to a lament for the paradise he would never reach.

One night, Meg came upon Roger in a clearing, the little life he had arrayed around himself—his Murakami books, his carefully folded shirts, bottles of grooming products lined up in the dirt—and she knew what had to be done.

"I've been thinking," she said, leaning against his shoulder.

"About what, beautiful Meg?"

"I think," she said, "we should take a trip to Big Sur."

They began the drive on a Friday morning. Meg had called in sick to the eye bank, and rented a car using the credit card she normally reserved for emergencies. Roger met her at the corner of Nineteenth and Lincoln. He climbed into the passenger seat, leaned over, and kissed her cheek.

"Oh, Meg, you have made me so happy," Roger said. "This is the kindest thing anyone has ever done for me."

"How does it work?" she asked. "Will it hurt, to be vaporized?"

"I do not know," Roger said. "I imagine it will be a great relief. I cannot wait for the burden of my memories to be removed."

As they drove south, they listened to the three David Bowie albums Meg had loved most in high school. Roger had never heard this music, and he kept turning up the volume, until the car's chassis rattled with sound.

"Meg, this song is about us!" he exclaimed, when he heard the chorus of "Kooks." " 'A couple of kooks, hung up on romancing'!"

She laughed. "Turn it down," she said. "You'll make me crash."

They stopped at a fruit stand near Gilroy. The temperature had risen ten degrees as they journeyed south, and Meg took off her sweatshirt and threw it in the backseat. They sat in the parked car with the windows rolled down, eating strawberries and candied almonds.

"Which memories do you want to forget?" Meg asked.

"It seems pointless to reflect on these events, now that I know they did not happen," Roger said. "They are not real."

"They're real to you, though," Meg said. She handed him the carton of strawberries, and he examined them before putting one in his mouth, stem and all.

"Yes," Roger said, chewing the strawberry. "I do not understand why they gave me such terrible memories, when they could have given me pleasant ones." He thought again of the murdered owl. How its babies had cried out from their nest.

"Probably so you could better relate to people," Meg said. "People like me."

"Do you have painful memories, Meg?"

"Of course," she said. "Everyone does."

"Would you like to recount some of them to me?"

"What's there to recount?" she said. "One day the people you love are alive. The next day, they're gone forever."

"Murakami wrote that death is not the opposite of life, but an innate part of it," Roger said.

Meg nodded. "That's very true."

"I know the feeling of wanting a home to return to," Roger said.

"Yes," Meg said. "I imagine you do." She pushed the button that brought the car back to life.

"Meg, would you like me to drive the rest of the way?"

She thought of the road ahead, which she remembered grew more winding and precipitous as they entered Big Sur. "Do you have a license?"

"No, and I have never operated a vehicle," Roger said. "But I possess an intrinsic knowledge of these roads. This is the path I was always meant to take."

She imagined their rental car careening over the cliffs and

bursting into flame. But as she regarded Roger's smiling face, she felt certain he would not lead them to such an end. It occurred to her that she trusted him more than anyone, even Genevieve. The way he would hurt her was already known, coded into his design at the cellular level. Everything else was left to fate, the random tragedy that could befall them regardless of who was driving.

Meg switched places with Roger, and he eased the car back onto the road. She gazed out the passenger window at the bright expanse of the Pacific. Her cellphone lost service, Spotify cutting out in the middle of *Low*'s final track. She leaned her seat back and drifted to sleep, lulled by Roger's capable handling of the curves.

Roger drove them to the cabin, located down several twisting back roads. It was a complicated path, but he was compelled by instinct, as birds understood where to migrate in winter. He had thought about this route every night, was able to picture it, and the cabin that lay at its end, with perfect clarity, though he had never been here before. Soon, they were upon it: a two-story cabin set into a hill that rose from the woods. He parked in the driveway, got out, and located a key beneath the third stone lining the path to the front door.

"Wow, this place is amazing," Meg said. She figured the cabin would cost at least five hundred a night on Airbnb. The granite-tiled foyer opened to a main room filled with live edge furniture; woven tapestries hung on the walls. In the kitchen, she found a long butcher block island, at the end of which sat a bowl of rotting fruit. The fridge was filled with food, much of it expired: goat milk yogurt, bottles of beer, restaurant leftovers gathering mold in their compostable clamshells. Upstairs, the bed was made up with a linen duvet. A deck opened off the bedroom, overlooking the ocean.

Meg wondered how previous blots had persuaded women to bring their laptops on the trip, even when there would be no Wi-Fi. She was glad she and Roger did not have to engage in such deceit. She'd brought her laptop without his asking, understanding what was required of her. She set it on the glazed tree stump that served as a bedside table.

Roger found her there, sitting on the edge of the bed. He'd been showering, and now wore a white bathrobe she imagined other blots had worn before him. "Beautiful Meg," he said, standing over her and brushing the hair from her forehead. "What should we do tonight?"

Impulsively, she grabbed his arm, pulling him down onto the mattress beside her.

They went to a restaurant set into the cliffs off the main road. They sat on the same side of a table on an outdoor patio, flanked by heat lamps shaped like trees. They ordered oysters, burgers and fries, a bottle of red wine. With some grooming, Roger had been restored to the handsomeness he'd possessed on the night she met him at the dinner party. Meg no longer felt embarrassed by his odd manner with the servers, his desire to always be touching her.

"Will it happen tonight?" Meg said, as they picked at the remaining fries.

"Either tonight or tomorrow night," Roger said. "I do not know which."

"If you're still here tomorrow, we should go on a hike," Meg said.

"I would like that very much," Roger said.

Roger was quieter than usual. He seemed to have settled into himself, and Meg realized that prior to this time, he must have been racked with a painful longing to arrive at Big Sur. Now that he was close to achieving his purpose, they were able to be present with each other. They stopped at a scenic overlook on the drive back to the cabin. Roger helped Meg climb the sand dunes off the parking lot. They slid over them, laughing, before collapsing into the sand. There was a new moon, and the darkness allowed the stars to stand in sharp relief, brighter than they ever could be in the city.

Back in the cabin, they had sex again. This sex had a different quality than before, slow and exploratory, each transaction defined by Meg's awareness that it would never be repeated. They both came eventually, then lay with their bodies entwined, the white sheets gritty with sand.

"I don't want to fall asleep," Meg whispered.

"You must, Meg," Roger said. "Sleep is essential for bodily and mental health."

"Once I fall asleep, I might never see you again," Meg said. She thought maybe if she stayed awake, she could keep Roger with her longer, at least one more day.

"There is another Murakami quote that I have been thinking about," Roger said. " 'If you remember me, then I don't care if everyone else forgets.' "

Meg began crying, silently, the tears forming a wet patch on the linen beneath her cheek. She didn't think Roger would notice, but he tightened his arms around her. "Do not cry,

Meg," he said softly. "I will always remember this day we've spent together. It has been the best day of my entire life."

His words comforted her, as they contained an implicit promise that Roger would continue existing, in some form. She understood that this was his purpose, his destiny, that standing in the way of it would do neither of them any good. She fell asleep in his arms, and slept better than she had in months. When she woke in the morning he was gone, the air in the room suffused by a fresh lavender scent.

She rolled over to the tree stump and opened her laptop, hoping to find some message from Roger, a love note scrawled in a Word document. But there was nothing. Later, when she was back in cell service, Meg would check her phone and find a photo Roger had sent the night before—at 8:35 P.M., when she had been in the bathroom at the restaurant—of a cocker spaniel wearing a straw panama hat. The message had gone through on Roger's end, meaning that wherever he and his phone had vanished to, there was cell service. She replied with a heart emoji, hoping he would respond, but hours and days passed, and he never did. She would keep texting Roger for years, even after she had begun dating the man she would marry and moved to a suburb of Seattle, where they started a family. She wanted to keep him updated, hoping that wherever he was, whatever blot hive mind he'd been absorbed into, some ember of his consciousness could still see her messages, even if he could never respond.

Meg made coffee from some stale grounds she found in the kitchen cupboard. She went on a long hike, and finally, as the sun drew low over the sea, began the journey north to reassemble her life.

Acknowledgments

All my thanks to my agent, Emma Patterson, for believing in my work and remaining my tireless advocate. Thank you to my editors, Clio Seraphim and Kwaku Osei-Afrifa, and their teams at Random House and Hodder Studio, for making the dream of this book into a reality.

These stories benefited from the feedback of my peers in the Stegner fiction workshop: Georgina Beaty, Brendan Bowles, Jamel Brinkley, Neha Chaudhary-Kamdar, Lydia Conklin, Evgeniya Dame, Devyn Defoe, Matthew Denton-Edmundson, Asiya Gaildon, Sterling HolyWhiteMountain, Nicole Caplain Kelly, Jamil Jan Kochai, Fatima Kola, and Gothataone Moeng. Thanks also to James Cotter, Brigid M. Hughes, Evan Karp, Lisa Locascio, David Mendoza, Ploi Pirapokin, and Joel Tomfohr for your friendship and support.

I'm grateful for my professors, especially Stephen Beachy, David Booth, Lewis Buzbee, Adam Johnson, Chang-rae Lee, and Elizabeth Tallent, for teaching me new ways of thinking about writing. I'm also grateful to Claire Boyle, Laura Cogan, Willing Davidson, and Oscar Villalon for their editorial guidance and championing of my work.

The completion of this book was aided by the generosity of the Headlands Center for the Arts, MacDowell, Stanford University, the Vermont Studio Center, and the Virginia Center for the Creative Arts.

Thanks above all to my parents, for telling me stories.

ABOUT THE AUTHOR

KATE FOLK has written for publications including *The New Yorker, The New York Times Magazine, Granta, McSweeney's Quarterly Concern,* and *Zyzzyva.* She's received support from the Headlands Center for the Arts, MacDowell, the Vermont Studio Center, and the Virginia Center for the Creative Arts. Recently, she was a Wallace Stegner Fellow in fiction at Stanford University. She lives in San Francisco. *Out There* is her first book.

katefolk.com
Twitter: @katefolk
Instagram: @kate__folk

ABOUT THE TYPE

This book was set in Walbaum, a typeface designed in 1810 by German punch cutter J. E. (Justus Erich) Walbaum (1768–1839). Walbaum's type is more French than German in appearance. Like Bodoni, it is a classical typeface, yet its openness and slight irregularities give it a human, romantic quality.